Erin Rise

Erin's story begins where Jasper and the Salamander ends.
And this time, she is all grown up.

J. J. Caler

Erin Rise

Her story begins

Published by J. J. Caler, 2024

Table of Contents

ERIN RISE
J. J.
CALER

Preface

Erin Rise is a historical fantasy novel that follows the adventures of Erin, a young woman who discovers her true identity and powers as the granddaughter of Aphrodite, the goddess of love.

Set in 1945, the novel blends elements of Greek mythology, time travel, and the strength of women, as Erin joins forces with her parents, Jasper and Maeve, and their crew of spirited ex-pirates, to stop the Nazis from unleashing a dark force that could destroy the world.

Along the way, Erin faces overwhelming change, danger and betrayal, as she learns to control her abilities and make her place in a time of war and chaos.

Erin Rise is the second book in the series that began with Jasper and the Salamander, but it can also be read as a standalone novel. It is a thrilling and captivating story that explores the themes of family, identity, and power, and how they are shaped by history and destiny.

J. J. Caler

Erin Rise

Chapter 1: A Spark of Discord

Berlin, Germany.
April 30, 1945

THE OLD MAN SAT IN the car, waiting. Sirens were blaring out in the streets, and the sound of distant gunfire pushed up the tempo of his heartbeat. He could smell the smoke and the blood in the air, and he wondered how many lives would be lost in this war.

"How long is she going to take?"

He held his gold watch up and looked at the time, then put it to his ear and smiled, listening to the tiny chimes sing their quiet ballad. It was a gift from Jasper, his captain. From the day he met Maeve hiding in his cabin on the Salamander.

Joey always admired the captain's watch. And you could tell if Jasper had an idea coming together because that watch would just be flipping and clicking open then closed.

Jasper noticed his admiration for the timepiece and had arranged to have one ordered and inscribed. Then he sent Joey to pick it up and have it wrapped and bring it back to his cabin. Joey was over the moon when the captain handed the small package back to him and said it was for him.

Inside, behind the heavy steel door and thick concrete walls of the bunker, Eris slipped through the halls, whispering into the ears of the men and women who hid inside. She enjoyed sowing seeds of doubt and fear among her enemies. She told them lies and truths, twisted and mixed them together until they were ready to do what she wanted them to do.

He watched her slip through the door like a ghost, a somewhat evil grin on her face. She walked toward him like a model on a runway and pointed next to the door and spoke quietly, "Set them here."

Joey took another look into the mirror and around the car. "Finally," he thought to himself. He felt like an open target, but he was glad to get this part over with and get back out of this city and over the American lines.

He got out of the car and opened the trunk, pulling out two green fuel cans, then sat them next to the heavy door where she indicated.

He had a fake press pass around his neck and he was wearing a pair of horn-rimmed glasses that made him look like a harmless old reporter. He had learned to blend in and play different characters over the years, but this was his most dangerous role yet. Right at the dragon's den.

Eris slid into the passenger seat and waited as Joey got behind the wheel. As if she really needed a ride. She was only there to make sure he got out safely. She could teleport herself anywhere she wanted, but she liked to keep an eye on him. She seemed to have a soft spot for him, probably the most non-chaotic and undramatic person in their group.

They took one last look at the thick concrete walls and heavily fortified steel that hid the scourge of man below. Joey could only imagine what she had been doing down there, but he knew the world would soon be rid of the world's worst mustache and the utter piece of trash that it grew out of.

Joey ground the transmission into gear, and they pulled away.

Watching out the windshield he could see the long red banners with their cult like rune hanging down from tall buildings. Symbols of oppression and hatred, and he hated them with every fiber of his being.

He rammed the lever into another gear, thinking, "No, they won't pull this piece of garbage out of his hiding place and let him live, because they don't want to set a bad precedent. Eris would make sure of that."

His internal conversation kept his mind away from worrying about how they were going to cross nearly a hundred miles back to the lines. He had a map and a plan. But most important, he had Eris.

Joey glanced at the young woman in the seat beside him, dressed like she was coming from the theater and was playing the part of a Greek goddess. Beige linen tunic, adorned with gold and silver Jewelry in all the right places to emphasize her charm. She was very attractive. And she was the deadliest person in this city right now.

Her eyes sparkled with mischief and malice, and her lips curved into a wicked smile. She had a dagger hidden in her belt and kept a necklace of skulls to wear around her neck. She was the embodiment of chaos and strife. How could he not love her for that?

She would have stuck out like a sore thumb, were it not for the fact that Joey was the only one around here that could see her. She liked to keep him company, and to tease him with her words and gestures. She told him that she was his goddess, and he was her mortal toy. She would start to play with him soon. When they reached the first check station, she would start asking him questions or telling him some nonsensical thing to try to distract him or make him talk to her and look foolish.

But between now and then, she would guide him around the broken streets of Berlin and keep him from being killed by a sniper or trapped in a dead end.

Eris vanished out of the car, gone. Someplace up ahead in the buildings was a short scream and a body falling from a window. Then another on the other side. And then she was there beside him again. He just kept driving along and looked for her to drop back in. He had slowly gotten used to her doing her own thing. He was glad she didn't use her tricks on him.

She told him to turn right as they approached a side street. He turned, and down the lane ahead was an SS soldier aiming a rifle straight at him.

And then she was beside the nasty bastard. She whispered in his ear, and he dropped his rifle and started dancing with her.

Joey just kept driving toward them. Eris smiled at him, then grabbed the fellow by his neck and gave him a fling up into the wall of the building on the left.

He fell to the ground into a lump and Eris was sitting next to him grinning again.

"We probably didn't even need to take this street." Joey commented to her.

"No, probably not. But I need to keep occupied or I get bored on these long drives."

Yeah, she was a sure nutcase. But she was our nutcase. And we loved her.

They made the edge of the city and started down a long road dotted with people trying to get away from the battle taking place behind them. The Russian troops were pushing into Berlin and would soon be in control.

ADOLPH SAT AT HIS DESK, both his arm and leg tremoring. He threw another pill into his mouth and washed it down.

Eva was lying on her side on the sofa, below the portrait of Fredrick the Great. "A true believer," He thought to himself.

He assessed his life's rewards around him. A desk, a bookcase, a sofa, and a portrait. And, of course, Eva. He had created his own reality and now it was all caving in on him. His armies had failed. The communists were at the gates. And he and his most faithful were trapped in this cramped, damp grave.

He opened a drawer and lifted out a small tin container. Lifting the lid, there were rows of white pills layered in wax paper. The odor of almonds reached his nose.

"Eva. Here, take some of these. It will calm you from the noise out there."

Eva got up obediently, holding out her hand. Adolph poured a glass of water from his pitcher as she put the pills into her mouth. He handed the drink to her, "There, you will feel relaxed soon."

He walked to the door, noting the water that was seeping in all around the edges of the floor. He looked into the conference room. There were a few of his men there, and they said a few words and he shook some hands and went back into his study.

He sat next to Eva and tossed several of the smelly pills into his own mouth and washed them down.

Then he began ranting about how he alone would have reversed the decline of civilization. How the world had betrayed him.

Eva listened for a few minutes, but then she began to moan in pain. She grabbed her stomach with both hands. She looked at his face, realizing what he had done to her. Her face contorted and she began to foam at her lips.

Hitler, seeing how painful her death was, immediately regretted taking the pills. He could not die in this painful way. He couldn't be found with his face looking like Eva's. And with his pants filled with his own excrement.

He felt the burning and stabbing inside him begin. His eyes darted around the room. There was nothing there for him. He couldn't stop what he set into motion.

He felt his Luger on his hip, pulled it out and fired it into his temple.

His body fell back onto the sofa, his wife's corpse beside him.

OUTSIDE THE SMALL STUDY, others heard the shot. His driver was sitting in the conference room, waiting for them. He had only been called a short time before to come and take Adolph and Eva to an airfield so they could escape the Russians.

He walked to the door and stood there, dreading opening it. What had happened? What changed? They were going to go far away and rebuild and start over.

He opened the door and found his Fuhrer sprawled back on the sofa with a hole in his temple.

He took a step back and nearly stepped on Goebbels' foot.

"He killed himself."

Joseph didn't say a word. He turned and went to his own small room.

There was a buzz of activity around the conference room. Some people were being rushed out of the bunker, up the stairs into the garden outside. Others were going into their damp concrete quarters like Goebbels had.

Joseph handed his wife his own tin of pills after removing a few for himself. He swallowed hard and took a drink of water.

As he sat down and waited, she turned to her six children.

A nurse was sitting in a chair, holding the smallest.

"No, not them. What are you doing?"

"I belong to my husband. And the children belong to me," Magda said.

The nurse tried to plead with her, but finally Magda forced her out of the room and shut the door.

Nobody liked Hitler. He was the lightning rod. He had the people convinced and he could say or do what they wanted but without any consequences. They just tied themselves to him so they could reap the benefits of power and money.

But now he was gone. Now there was no curtain to hide behind. All of the lies melted away like a sheet of ice suddenly exposed to the warm sun.

Magda poisoned the baby last, it being least likely to put up any complaint. Then she took her own. Sat down beside her family and thought about how the world had betrayed them all. Why couldn't they accept what she knew was right? The Reich could have lasted a thousand years.

"LOOK AT THEM, ERIS. Look at all these poor souls. They have nothing left but their lives, and even those they might not have for long."

Joey felt empathy for the people who struggled down the road and looked at them as they passed with no hope left in their eyes.

"I see them, Joey. I see their fear and their despair. And I also see their guilt and shame. They bet on a madman, and now they will pay the price."

Eris did not share his empathy. How many millions of people had she seen just like this smile over the tormented body of another. Stand laughing at their humiliation and destruction. Fifty million dead since they put that man in power. They all had their motivations. Something they thought they would gain.

"Not all of them, Eris. Some of them were just innocent bystanders, caught in the crossfire. Some of them were forced to obey, or to keep silent. Some of them tried to resist, or to help others. You can't judge them all by the same standard."

"Maybe not, Joey. But you can't deny that they all share the responsibility for what happened here. For the millions who died, for the atrocities that were committed, for the war that ravaged the world. They all have blood on their hands, Joey. And so do we."

"What do you mean, Eris? We're not like them. We're not Nazis. We're not killers. We're here to stop the evil, not to spread it."

"Oh, Joey. You're so naive. We're not heroes, Joey. We're not saviors. We're just pawns in a bigger game. A game that's been played for centuries, by forces that you can't even comprehend. A game that has no winners, only losers."

Eris paused and gave Joey a serious look before she continued.

"And those men and their wives and children we just left behind in the bunker. They are definitely going to die. And I definitely made sure they would. And you helped me do it. You mortals are fairly loose on your definition of killers. I know what I am."

"What are you talking about, Eris? Are you getting philosophical on me again?" Joey gave his head a little bit of a tilt as he looked at her, as if he was putting a question mark on his sentence.

"It has always been the game of the gods, Joey. The forces of Olympus, of Asgard, of Egypt, of Babylon, of every pantheon that ever existed. They're all here, Joey. They're all watching. They're all meddling. They're all fighting. For power, for glory, for revenge. And we're just their tools, Joey. Their weapons. Their toys."

"That's not true, Eris. You're one of them, Eris. You're a goddess. You're not like them. You're different. You're good."

"Am I, Joey? Am I good? Or am I just playing the role I was given this time, like you? A role that suits my nature, my purpose, my destiny. A role that I couldn't escape, even if I wanted to. A role that I was born to play. Athena could have done this job. Aphrodite could have. Even Erin could have, if someone let her in. But here I am, aren't I? I know who I am. It's just the way it is."

She put her hand on Joey's shoulder and leaned over to him a little.

"Today, we make the world better. Today we end a cancer on the soul of man. Tomorrow? Maybe I ignite the flames of destruction. Tomorrow, maybe I make the world burn, Joey."

Joey pushed her hand off his shoulder, "God, stop that. You know that creeps me out when you get all 'duality' on me."

Eris leaned back and laughed at him.

She wasn't lying to him. Not one bit. Joey didn't dare add up the lives lost in the fort they attacked from the Salamander. How many went to the deep on the thirteen ships they at least helped to sink, if they didn't sink wholly themselves in the aftermath.

He was on the Salamander, and he was part of the crew. He played his role and believed in his captain. Just like Eris plays her role and believes in hers.

We men like to find excuses. We need to justify the things we do when they don't fit into our version of morality. We had to do it to survive. She simply is what she is. She could level the entire city they had left behind if she were told to do it. And she doesn't hide from it.

No, they were different. A goddess and a man. But they were the same too. Characters in some cosmic play, being performed eon after eon. The ending never changes, because it never truly ends.

They were within a few miles of Magdeburg and the American lines. Eris pointed to the side of the road, "Pull over there. We need to walk from here."

Joey steered up onto a gentle bank and shut off the engine. He looked into the mirror and started removing his makeup and revealing the much younger Joey that was hidden beneath, throwing remnants of fake hair and flesh-colored bits he had pasted to his face into the back seat. He poured some water onto a cloth and wiped himself down to get any remaining makeup off.

They both got out and he tossed the keys back inside on the seat.

"Maybe some of them can use a ride." he indicated shifting his head back toward Berlin.

He started to walk away.

"They probably could." Eris smiled, then she put her hand inside the car and the seats burst into flames, "But we won't give them one."

"You can seem downright cruel sometimes, Eris."

"I can't believe you would say something like that about me, Joey," She grinned and tilted her head like a puppy, "I am nothing if not kind, generous and charitable." She walked up next to him and put her arm around his shoulder, "To you."

Her smile was beaming across her face.

Joey jerked out from under her arm, "Argh! You just love toying with my affections don't you."

"I really do."

Joey tried to make his steps put some space between them.

"I had grown content with the fact that I was going to die old and alone, now I am starting to think that Zeus intends to torment me with you forever instead." Joey grumbled.

"Hey, that is something we should look into more." Eris ran over next to him and grabbed his hand.

"Hey, maybe we shouldn't" Joey shrugged her away.

"Imagine it, Joey," she said as she kept pace and looked at him, "I could cast the water from the sea, and we could have a candlelight dinner on the ocean floor together."

"And then race to see if we could escape before the water came back, and one of us doesn't have to use their legs, do they?" He cut back at her.

"You are always seeing the negatives, Joey."

"Plus, I am not sure if I could come to terms with how 'murdery' you are."

"Like I said, only focus on the negative. You would get used to it in no time at all. Not like we would run out of time anytime soon."

Joey kept walking, it would be a mile or two to the checkpoint. He took a little peek at Eris every now and then.

He didn't want her to see him do it though. Of course, he likes her. She was a little crazy, well, whole lot crazy. But she had his back. She was clever beyond anyone. She had a hilarious sense of humor when they were together. And her looks were captivating.

But he couldn't see her attentions as anything more than just playing with him. She was a goddess, and he was a ship's watchman and a wood carver and most recently a play actor and general set hand at the theater.

He enjoyed a quiet simple life, and she was literally the goddess of chaos. But my lord was she fun. Joey always pushed back on her, but he wouldn't waste a breath if it were real.

It was going to take some time to figure out this whole goddess and mortal man thing. And he wasn't even sure how mortal he was anymore. Just a few months ago he was in his fifties. Then Jasper was all like, 'Joey, do you want to help us save the world?' and boom, flash, zip, thirty years gone.

He still hadn't sorted all of that out, and now he has this reddish haired and blue-eyed vixen toying with his heart strings.

The guard stationed up the road started to come into view, and Joey sidestepped over next to Eris and took her hand.

"Eris, please, please, please, will you behave this time?"

"Well, what about that seafloor dinner for two?" she spoke in her buttery quiet voice.

"So, I have to agree to let you drown me to get a little relief?"

"I would never drown you. I can't believe you would think that of me."

Joey looked at her, and verified her evil grin was present.

"There is no hope for me. All is lost." He let her hand go, and trudged on to what he knew was coming.

They reached the checkpoint, where a group of Allied soldiers were guarding the road. Joey walked up to them, hoping to pass through without any trouble.

"Hello there, sir. What's your business here?" one of the soldiers asked.

"Hello. I'm a journalist, and I'm here to cover the end of the war. I have a press pass and a camera, if you want to see them." Joey said, showing his fake credentials.

Eris put her hands around his neck. "You're so good at lying, Joey. You should be an actor."

Joey felt a shiver down his spine and tried to ignore her.

The G.I. looked at Joey with a puzzled look. "What's that on your neck?"

Joey paused, then quickly pulled out a handkerchief. "Is that still there?" he asked as he wiped Eris's fingers. "It's just some garbage from back in the city. It's pretty bad back there. The Russians have advanced into the city, and they are taking it apart."

The soldier looked at the papers and nodded. "Alright, sir. You can go ahead. But be careful, it's still dangerous out there."

"Thank you. I appreciate it." Joey said, starting to walk again.

But Eris was not done with him yet. She reached over and grabbed his hand, squeezing it hard. "You know, Joey, I really like you. You're so brave and loyal. And handsome, too."

Joey felt a rush of pain and anger and tried to pull his hand away. He looked at her with a glare and whispered back.

"Eris, stop it. You're hurting me. And you're making me look suspicious. Let go of me."

Eris smiled and shook her head. "No, Joey. I won't let go of you. I want to hold you. I want to kiss you. I want to make love to you."

Joey tried to force a smile as he walked past another group of young soldiers. Hoping they didn't notice him biting his lip.

Eris kept clinging to his hand and touching him. Delighting in his torment.

Finally, in what seemed like forever they hit a clear spot.

"My god, you are really going to get me killed or locked up."

"I would never let them hurt you, you know that." Eris smiled smugly.

"Well, I don't want you killing off half of the allied soldiers to save me, either." Joey freed his hand from her grip and held it up to his chest rubbing it with the other.

Eris looked at Joey like she had just had an epiphany. "Maybe that is what I really like about you, Joey. You would never try to use me as a weapon or to gain power. You're just Joey, and we really are becoming good friends, aren't we."

Joey looked at her, still somewhat annoyed. And he noticed something in Eris that he hadn't seen in her before. Sincerity.

"Yes, Eris. You are a very good friend. And I am glad to be yours."

She practically skipped closer to him and took his hand again, much more gently this time. "Good. I like my friend Joey. I think we are going to have a lot of fun together."

Joey didn't try to push her away this time. He guessed that the camera case hanging from that hand would keep anyone from noticing he was holding onto an invisible goddess. And she was content, so he was content.

Chapter 2: The Cove of Evermore

The east coast of Brazil.
1926

JASPER CUT THE ENGINES and the small craft glided forward into the calm waters of their forgotten paradise. He lifted his hat and dabbed the sweat from his forehead. They only lived here for three years, but it felt like coming home.

Erin was leaning over the railing, and he could sense her excitement from the ship's helm. He hummed a little tune to himself as he steered the final stretch. It looked much like the first time they sailed beneath the archway. The jungle had reclaimed itself.

Scenes of sand
and the arms of palms
and mandrakes reaching high,
shadows passing by.

With painted birds
singing words
and the wings drift between
a breathless sky.

Our sails are set
on the eastern shore
under shelter of the runes,
Of the Queen of Light.

In the Cove of Evermore.

HER PARENTS HAD TOLD her about this place so many times. They claimed she was born here, right on the water in the captain's cabin of a ship they called the Salamander. That isn't what her birth certificate said, but she had no reason not to believe them.

It really was just as they described. A large hidden lagoon with huge cliff walls protecting the entrance. It led in from the sea through a tall archway with carvings above. There was a huge rift in the rock directly at the center over the arch. And there were runes chiseled into the rock all around the tops of the cliffs. Archaeology was kind of a big deal back in Lyme Regis. And she had the benefit of seeing runes in textbooks. She wondered what secrets these held. And who were the people who put them there?

The water was clear, and she watched a rainbow of fish swimming right beneath her. They sparkled and changed colors in the light. They were like an open pirate's chest filled with jewels, waiting for her to dive into the depths and retrieve them.

The lagoon itself was shaped in a long crescent. It made part of the shore almost appear as an island, jutting out into the water. The sandy beach reached its long hand into the cove offering a nice effortless walk from the shore into the deeper water.

Eris took it all in, holding the rail expecting the jolt of the hull as it nosed into the white sand.

Maeve held Jasper around his waist, as she watched her daughter from across the deck.

"Fourteen years, Jasper. There have been a lot of days I wished we had never left here." She leaned the side of her face into his back.

"Fourteen or two hundred and what? Four?" Jasper turned to take her into his arms.

"Can I swim?" Eris called them from the side of the deck. Anxious to get off the small cruiser and get her balance under her own control again.

Both Jasper and Maeve looked carefully into the water.

"Well, can I?" She persisted impatiently.

"Did you see anything?" Jasper asked Maeve.

"No, nothing bad."

"Okay," Jasper answered, "But remember what we told you and don't go out too far from the shore. Things can change in the water fast."

"Yes, I know..." Eris broke into the almost silly poem they had made her remember.

Frogs, spiders, ants and snakes
All looking for a life to take
Cats and caiman hide and wait
To devour flesh until their hunger sate
Piranha and sharks with tearing teeth
Wait and watch in the water beneath
And eels that shock you hide in the deep
To take your soul to Hades' keep

JASPER WAVED FOR HER to go ahead, and she dove from the side of the deck, barely breaking the quiet all around them with her delicate splash. She slid back to the surface, then rinsed a pair of goggles and slipped them over her eyes.

She completely lost track of everything around her now, mainly, her parents. She dove below and challenged her lungs as she held her breath longer and longer each time.

The tiny fish came up to her and gave her little kisses. She would hold out her hands and watch them swim across and around her palms. She would swim forward, and they would follow her like she was part of their school.

The couple watched as their amazing daughter glided through the water. Both imagining how it would be if they had never left that fateful day. Enduring what came after made it easy to forget the feelings of boredom and the lack of direction everyone was feeling then. The monotony that had started to take over their lives.

But it was good to be here today. It was good to bring Erin back and remember the place she was born. To look at each other and recall the feelings they had that day and the excitement of the crew outside the cabin. Long forgotten Nara and her chosen Tom.

"I wonder how they did, Maeve? Tom and Nara." Jasper asked.

"I am sure they did better than we did. At least for the first while." She smiled at him.

"You really haven't set the bar very high there." Jasper gave her a little chuckle.

"Let's build a fire, Jasper. Let's sit down here tonight and tell stories like Blejack and John did."

"Hopefully we can keep Erin still and in one place long enough. I think that is a great idea. I wonder if she would like pirate stories?"

"Hey, she isn't ready for our story yet. She will think we are both crazy." Maeve reminded him. He had brought up telling her the truth of their lives before this. But his wife was right. It was too unbelievable and crazy.

They built a fire and walked along the beach, recalling where huts were and the stage that John had built. Blejack's personal floor for his rocking chair. Her private bathing pool. It was all long gone. But it was in their mind like it was just yesterday.

They sat by the fire that night and Jasper recounted the story of the naval battle after the fort raid and the Battle of Shadows, leaving out some key points and characters. Maeve wouldn't let him tell the whole story, but he insisted on telling what she would let him.

Two more days in paradise. It was an amazing place, this hidden harbor they were led into so many years ago as their temporary home to hide from the authorities. An amazing and dangerous place.

Well after the sun had set, they put the fire out and went back aboard the small ship. It had a low deck with railings all the way around it, and a large cabin took up most of it, leaving a walkway on the perimeter. The front and sides had large windows so you could see the interior from outside, the wheel and instruments at the front, and a sitting area behind it.

Inside, there were small sleeping berths and a restroom with a shower at the rear. It wasn't the captain's cabin on the Salamander, but it brought back the memory of their home. Gently rocking on the placid waters of the lagoon.

The following day, Erin was right into the water. Jasper and Mave watched her from the deck, eating a small breakfast.

"We should show her the forest, Maeve."

"Yes, we definitely should. She will love that." She looked at her husband with a huge smile.

"Well, go get dressed and I will get her out of the water."

Jasper overcame Erin's resistance and got her back into her own cabin to change and then she walked out onto the deck wearing a long blue officer's coat she had pillaged from her mother's closet. Jasper froze and stared at her. She was only a few years younger now than Maeve was when he met her. She had worn that coat many times. And he felt like he was looking at her again through time.

Erin looked at him, seeing his eyes glossing up, ready to set free a tear, "Dad, are you okay?"

"Oh, yes, never better. You are a mirror image of your mother. It is almost too much for an old man's heart."

Erin hugged her dad, "Aww, you are such a sap, daddy."

"Only for you two. I will always be your sap."

Maeve came out and smiled at the father and daughter. She watched them holding each other silently for a few minutes and then, against the protest from her own heart, she interrupted them.

"I hate to break up this moment for you two, but we had better go before the day slips away." They set off into the tall palms and shrubs.

And it was a stunning day for them all. The animals used to dart away and hide. You would only get a glimpse of them. But today, they sat in trees or on the shrubs and watched. Chirping and cackling and making all kinds of noises. Neither Jasper nor Maeve had ever seen this side of the forest. It felt like they had come to see Erin. Maybe there was a kinship because she was actually born right there in the lagoon. She was part of their jungle.

They hiked through the wood for several hours then returned to the soft sands of the beach. Maeve started preparing a late lunch and Erin walked along the shore, exploring the edges of the lagoon.

"We could come back, Jasper. We could just stay. We could do it again. Live right here. Look at her. Look how happy and peaceful she is. And we would be so far from all the chaos of the world."

Jasper walked behind her and wrapped her into his arms from behind, resting his chin on her head.

"I don't think we can ever go back. Sometimes I wish for it so hard I can feel my heart breaking. Then I remember this place has teeth too. It's like a jaguar lying in the sun. So beautiful, and so at rest and peaceful. Then you put your hand out to pet it and it tries to tear away everything you are."

Maeve peered back at him, giving him a look that let him know he was bursting her bubble and then went back to cooking.

THE NEXT MORNING, ERIN didn't wait for anyone else to wake up. She sat down on the floor and looked through her things, finding a large sketch pad and a wooden box filled with pencils and graphite sticks.

She had brought them with her to help pass the time while traveling. And she was a fair sketch artist.

She opened the wooden box and took out a graphite stick and a water brush. She flipped through the sketch pad until she found a blank page. She decided to draw a map of the area, marking the location of the cliffs and the runes. She had been fascinated by the ancient symbols since they arrived, and she wanted to learn more about them.

She quickly sketched the outline of the land and the water, using the graphite stick to create some shading and contrast. Then she added some color with the water brush, using the watercolor paint set that was attached to the lid of the box. She used blue for the sea, green for the grass, and brown for the rocks. And as an afterthought, added an "X" where their boat was moored.

She smiled as she looked at her map. It was not very accurate or detailed, but it captured the essence of the place. She wrote the date and the name of the location on the corner of the page. She then closed the sketch pad and put the graphite stick and the water brush back into the box.

She grabbed her backpack and slung it over her shoulder. She also took a small pair of scissors and some adhesive tape from the box and put them in her pocket. She was ready to go.

She tiptoed out of the cabin, careful not to wake up her parents. She had told them she was going for a walk, but she didn't mention anything about the cliffs or the runes. She knew they would worry or try to stop her. They didn't understand her curiosity and passion for adventure.

She slipped off the boat and headed towards the cliffs. She could see them from a distance, towering over the clear aqua-blue water. She bubbled with excitement and anticipation. What secrets and mysteries were these runes hiding, and what stories could they tell? She couldn't wait to find out.

She walked around the edge of the forest, following the crescent shape of the beach. She had been keeping an eye out for a way up there. And she thought she spotted one when they were returning from their exploration the day before.

There was a small outcropping just above the waterline. She could walk to it if the tide were out, but it would be a short wade if not. And it looked like she was going to need to get wet this morning.

She lifted her pack and made the short trek across the water to the rocky side. She threw her pack up onto the ledge, then managed to wedge her toes and hands into a large crack and climb up.

She looked around as she slipped the backpack onto her arms. From here she could see what was hidden before. There was an opening behind the large extrusion of stone. And it looked like a pathway.

Taking a last glance at the boat where her parents were still sleeping, she hopped over the edge and onto the trail.

She ducked under a large section of rock and then it opened up above her. The path was a few feet wide and had a worn stone floor. It hadn't been used in years, probably hundreds of years. But, except for some areas with small piles of rock and dirt, it was clear enough for her to walk it.

She looked up at the cliff walls on both sides of her, reaching up thirty or forty feet. She would need to be watchful. There were plenty of wild things here that could be trouble. Snakes, mostly snakes. And frogs. Poison frogs. And spiders. Big murdery spiders.

She shook off a shiver and began moving farther into the unknown.

She walked for about half an hour, following the twists and turns of the trail. She saw some signs of life along the way, such as birds' nests, animal tracks, and colorful flowers. She also noticed some carvings on the walls, but they were too faded and eroded to make out. She stopped a few times and tried to make a rough sketch of what she could make out.

She reached a point where the trail split into two directions. She had to make a choice. She looked at the left path, which seemed to go up and around a bend. She looked at the right path, which seemed to go down and into a dark tunnel. She thought for a moment, then decided to go right. She had a feeling that the tunnel would lead her to something interesting.

She took out a flashlight from her backpack and turned it on. She entered the tunnel, which was narrow and low. She had to crouch and squeeze through some parts. She felt a cold breeze on her face and heard a faint sound of water dripping. She hoped there were no bats or rats in there.

She continued to walk through the tunnel, shining her flashlight on the walls and the floor. She saw some more carvings, but they were still too vague to decipher. She wondered how old they were, and who made them. She wished she had a camera or a sketchbook to document them.

She reached the end of the tunnel, which opened up into a large chamber. She gasped as she saw what was inside. There was a pool of water in the center, reflecting the light from a hole in the ceiling. The walls were covered with runes, carved in different shapes and sizes. They looked ancient and mysterious, and they glowed with a faint blue light.

Her heart pulsed with awe and excitement. She wasn't looking for this. But she had found runes. She couldn't believe her eyes. She wanted to touch them, to read them, to understand them. She walked towards the pool, careful not to slip or splash. She reached the edge and looked at the runes. They were beautiful and intriguing.

She took out a pencil and a piece of paper from her backpack. She started to trace some of the runes, hoping to decipher their meaning later. She felt a connection with them, as if they were speaking to her.

In her deep focus on her find, she lost herself. She went from one relief to the next, tracing and drawing. She had turned off and laid down her flashlight by her backpack. She could see perfectly in the eerie glow. And she was completely unaware of the blue lines tracing themselves around her body.

Erin felt a sudden jolt of pain in her head, as if the runes were trying to communicate with her. She dropped her pencil and paper and clutched her temples. She saw flashes of images and memories that were not her own, and she heard a voice in her mind.

It was the voice of an old man, weary and wise. He spoke in a language she didn't know, but somehow, she understood. He told her of a great battle that happened long ago. A battle between light and darkness, between good and evil. A battle that shaped the destiny of the world.

He showed her the scenes of the battle, as if she were there. She saw the armies in dark armor, marching in force, with fire and steel. She saw warriors riding through the shadows bringing terror and death.

He turned her eyes to the open land behind, brave men and women, fighting back. His people. They struggled, many falling to the field of battle. But they held.

She felt the emotions of the battle, as if she were part of it. She felt their fear and their pain, their anger and their sorrow. And then their joy and glory.

She hears the voice of the old man, telling her the meaning of the battle. He told her that it was not just a war of swords and spears, but a war of souls and spirits. It was not just a fight for land and wealth, but a fight for freedom and justice. It was not just a clash of kings and lords, but a clash of gods and fates.

He told her that the battle of evermore is not over but continues to this day. The runes are the legacy of the ancient ones, who fought and died for the cause of light. He told her that the runes are the guardians of the cove, where the secrets and treasures of the old world are hidden. The runes are the keys to the future, where the prophecy and the destiny of the new world are revealed.

He told her that she is the one, the one who can see and hear and understand the runes. He told her that she has a special gift, a gift of power and knowledge. He told her that she has a great responsibility, a responsibility for choice and action. She is the only one that can hold at the world's end.

He told her to remember, to learn, and to act. To be brave, to be wise, and to be good.

There would be a day when those she will put her trust in will try to mute her. To take her off the path of her destiny. That day, the cove would be waiting for her. For her to return here and to bring it back.

Erin notices that some of the runes are glowing brighter than others, and they seem to form a pattern. She follows the pattern, and it leads her to a hidden door in the wall.

The old man told her, "Go in. And remember."

She opened the door and found a secret chamber with more runes and artifacts. She saw a vision of a man wearing a strange pendant. A blue light began to radiate from its center.

He was wearing a hood and holding a sword. Another approached him and they did battle. This man was wearing bronze and silver armor.

The man in the hood fought, fending off blow after blow. But then he fell to the floor, pierced by the sword. His attacker leaned forward and took the pendant from his neck.

He disappeared leaving the dying man on the cold stone. Now she saw his face. It was the old man who had been showing her these visions.

Then the vision was gone, and before her was a skeleton.

He whispered one last thing to her, and then he faded away. "You must close the rift. Bring it back."

She opened her eyes, and she was alone in the cave. She looked at the runes, and they were silent and still. She looked at her watch, and she was shocked. She had been in the cave for hours, and the tide had risen. She had to find another way out or wait until the water receded.

She picked up her backpack and ran back to the tunnel, only to find that it was flooded. She was trapped in the cave, and she didn't know what to do. By now her parents would be worried.

She turned and went back into the cave and sat down, trying to sort all of this into someplace that made sense in her mind.

She wondered if the voice was real, or if it was a hallucination. She wondered if the battle was true, or if it was a fantasy. How could she be involved in any of this?

As she sat there shuffling her thoughts and trying not to worry about how she would get out of there and what her parents must be thinking right now, Aphrodite moved up behind her. Silent and invisible, she placed her hand on Erin's head and whispered something in some ancient language.

Erin woke up to her father and mother's voices, yelling for her. She sat up on the beach and looked back in their direction.

She furled her brow, "What am I doing here?" She looked at her watch, it was six pm. "Oh my god, I must have fallen asleep here."

She jumped up and yelled back to her parents, "I'm over here! I'm coming!"

She picked up her pack and ran back toward the boat and Jasper and Maeve.

Her parents ran toward her, "Where have you been? We were worried out of our minds. We have looked and called for hours."

"I am so sorry," she blurted out as they got closer. "I don't know how, but I just fell asleep on the beach. I don't even remember it."

ERIN HAD BEEN SWIMMING in these warm tropical waters of the lagoon for three days and she had seen so many radiant fish. Golds, yellows, purples and pinks. Every color of the rainbow. She could hold her breath for several minutes and swim below the gentle rippling of the breeze on the surface.

This time, there was something new. Something she had been told, warned about. It was like a snake with copper on its top and sides and white on the bottom. But she wasn't feeling afraid of it. It just swam near her and swished in the water looking at her. Her mind kept telling her she needed to back away and get out of the water, but she was captivated by how the eel just seemed curious and maybe even friendly.

Jasper and Maeve were sitting on the shore together, reminiscing and enjoying each other alone, a rare treat for the two of them. Completely unaware of the waltz under the surface.

Erin didn't think about it. She reached an open hand out to touch the prehistoric looking reptile on its nose.

Then there was a sudden burst of blue light and electricity in the water around both of them.

Erin's body jerked back, and she rolled face up, slowly drifting to the surface.

Jasper and Maeve saw her immediately, both running the few feet between them and the water and diving in for her.

They pulled Erin to shore, and Maeve started pumping her chest, Jasper blowing into her mouth.

It was only a second and Erin was spitting out a small bit of water and pushing her dad's face away from her own.

"Oh my god, stop, what are you two doing?" She burst out.

"Erin, you nearly died!" Maeve said, finding a voice someplace between crying and a scream of terror.

Jasper lifted Erin up, holding her tight.

"What happened, Erin?"

"I got distracted and thought I could pet an eel." She grinned. She was apparently unaffected by the entire incident.

Jasper looked into the water and saw the offending fish.

"You let him be, dad. He didn't mean any harm."

The eel was floating still below the surface, then it started to swish its long body and swim away.

"I think it hurt him more than it did me." Erin smiled at the eel as it disappeared to the other side of the lagoon.

THAT NIGHT, JASPER stood in her doorway, watching her sleep. She seemed unaffected by the near drowning earlier that day. She was at peace with the world, and they couldn't ask any more for their daughter. He closed the door and walked back across the small hall into the cabin with Maeve.

"How is she?"

"She is fine. Looks like the two of us took all the trauma from that one."

Maeve smiled and held her hands out to him.

"Well, come on then. You aren't doing any of us any good lurking around the ship all night."

He climbed into bed with her, pulling himself close to his reddish-haired princess with her hypnotizing blue eyes. 'Staying here forever would be just fine right now,' he thought to himself. Then he told Maeve softly, "Tomorrow we will leave out and go back to get the others."

"I know. I hate to have to say goodbye to this place again."

"I hope Tom and Nara had a great life and a dozen kids." Jasper was half smiling in the fond thought of them happy and also tormented by a dozen kids.

"Wow, a dozen, Jasper? I thought you liked them."

"Blessings, Maeve. Children are blessings."

"Oh, I agree. I can't even remember life before Erin. But there is such a thing as too much."

"I have a feeling Nara could have handled it. Tom, well, not without her."

"Okay, just shut up and let's go to sleep before you get any more wild ideas in that thick head of yours." Maeve rolled over toward the wall.

"Get?" Jasper whispered.

"No. She will wake up from the boat rocking. Go on to sleep."

Jasper laid back, enjoying his teasing, but pouting a little bit too.

Across the hall, Erin sleeps quietly, while traces of blue light draw patterns on her skin. Seeping through the slits in her eye lids. As she rests her body pulses with the power hiding inside her, still unaware of what she is.

Chapter 3: The Telling

Lyme Regis, England.
1914

WHEN JASPER DID FINALLY let it out, Joey, John, Paul and Blejack were all there. John gave us the full history and lowdown on Athena. Slipping in, unseen to mortals, guiding their hands, whispering into their ears to give them ideas and plans.

No, looking back, it was a good possibility there was some monkey business going on. Even for Joey, that was a lot of carving. And it usually wasn't his style to repeat his art-form.

He had carved every doorway and window frame with runes and glyphs. Many reminded the men of the ones on the arch leading into the lagoon. He had given this room in the theater the bonus treatment.

Athena was the goddess of wisdom, military leadership, and strategy. She could grant the power to devise clever and effective plans, to learn and master any skill, and to solve any problem. She was the goddess of craftsmanship. According to myth, she created the first ship.

She had a long reputation for putting herself into the destinies of mortal men. She favored the Greeks in their war on Troy. Athens was named for her, after all. They had many temples for her. But mainly, it was in her anger towards Aphrodite that she wanted to have Troy razed to the ground. And, well, she was Zeus's favorite daughter.

We had all heard the stories of the Iliad and the Odyssey many times in the lagoon. Watched the men create their play and narrate the story from the stage on the beach, and now we have seen them do it in the lights of our own theater, in dress costume and for a real audience.

Now, not saying I am superstitious or anything, but it is my best guess those glyphs were to protect Jasper, Maeve and Hannah. And, since we were all in the same places, the rest of us were protected as well. But we would all be targeted now.

Jasper agreed. And John, for such a book smart man, he didn't put up a fuss at all. Blejack was onboard from the start of it. We call him the witch doctor for a reason. Well, the main reason is his hair conditioner, but he does other stuff too. Like poisoning the captain when he is supposed to give him a nap.

Jasper went on to tell us how he had heard Aphrodite's whisper, and then began to remember her places that he had not noticed her before. Like the day he met Maeve in the Tavern. He was all but certain that after we were transported to the north Atlantic, she put the fog over us all that time to hide us from Ares while she begged Poseidon and Zeus to step in and stop Ares. It made sense, because as soon as the fog broke, that was when Ares came to him and tested him.

After that, there was no more fog, because he had passed the tests and Ares couldn't kill him. Kill, everything else was still on the table.

We were like a bunch of schoolboys, plotting out our fantasies. John said that Jasper's theory would track well with her history. She had used fogs or mists to remove men from the battlefield in the past. This was on a scale he had never read, but under the circumstances, it made sense why she would pull out all the stops.

John started making charts for the Greek gods. Mainly the ones that Jasper had already mentioned, but others as well. Establishing their skills, special abilities, rivalries, everything he could find. Blejack found himself joining in with him. He would show up with some new book or text and check and compare with John to see if there was anything new.

Then Blejack started making a book, storing the information. He listed the traits and assigned a number to each, depending on the amount of information he had and the supposed strength or weakness. He attempted to put drawings of them in the pages, but that got really sketchy, pardon the pun. Trouble with gods is, you see what they want you to see. They will appear as anyone, or not at all.

The not at all part Jasper emphasized. Do not speak about these things outside of the room. You don't know who is listening. That sent the witch doctor onto his next mission. Chasing down trinkets and charms. Who knows if any of them were any good. But if he brought you one, you took it and kept it. Seemed like it was better than nothing.

According to everything that they could find, Troy was the turning point. Aphrodite, Ares, Apollo and Artemis left Zeus and stayed in the mortal world. All felt betrayed that he had allowed Greece to win, and he did so because Athena was his favorite. They weren't wrong.

I won't bore you with a retelling of the Iliad, but here is the brief version of what started it. Hera, Zeus's wife, Athena, his daughter with Hera, and Aphrodite his daughter also, from another, had challenged him to choose who was the most beautiful. Well instead of doing the right thing and choosing his wife, he decided it was foolish to get trapped in that mess. So, he put it off onto Paris, the young prince of Troy.

Paris really wasn't interested in this contest either, so Eris was sent to give him a golden apple. It had some inscription on it like "the most beautiful" or something. So, then three goddesses all offered him some great prize if he picked them. Third in line was Aphrodite. She offered him Helen. The most beautiful woman on earth.

So, that set off the chain of events leading to the fall of Troy. When Zeus saw the war brewing below, he asked which of his underlings had been meddling. Hera and Athena both told Zeus it was Aphrodite's fault. And that she should be sent away.

Some stories say that Helen was also a daughter of Aphrodite, but it didn't say that in the Iliad, and we all accepted that as the definitive source and authority when it concerned Greek gods. And other texts mention that Eris was Aphrodite's daughter as well. Now that would make sense, seeing as how she has taken such an interest in Maeve and Erin. Imagine she was proud that they named the baby so closely to her own. In sound and spelling that is. Erin means 'Peace' and that really isn't Eris's strong suit.

Now the curious thing was, as Jasper told us his tales, and we got to the part where Maeve was Aphrodite's daughter, not one of us questioned it. Why, we just weren't surprised to hear that. She did require more study by us though. Not much. She was an amazing woman to look upon, sure. But it was her innate ability to connect with people.

Blejack started to make pages on her, to list her traits. Jasper smacked him right on the back of his head. "No! First of all, 'no'. And second, what if someone ever finds the book? I don't want anyone to analyze my wife, and I don't want anyone having an advantage over her either."

I 'think' that ended that. But you never know what Blejack does in the dark corners he hides in. He probably had a second book with all of us in it. Probably sat in his office at night throwing his dice and pitting us against his demons and dragons and sorcerers.

South of England. The English Channel.
1944

BLEJACK TAPS JASPER on the arm, "Hey, better come back to the present. They are here."

Jasper nodded to his cousin, "I am here. How does it look?"

Blejack was still looking through his binoculars at the other craft.

"Just two of them is all I can see on the deck."

"Well, let's bring them in and see what they have to show us."

Blejack lit the small, shaded lantern and let it swing in the predetermined pattern to tell the other boat to approach.

The other boat was a small fishing trawler, like the one that Jasper and Blejack were on. It had a wooden hull, a single mast, and a small cabin. It was painted in a dull gray color, blending in with the foggy and gloomy weather. It had a British flag flying from the stern, but Jasper knew that could mean nothing in these times.

The trawler slowly approached their boat, keeping a safe distance. Jasper could see the two men on the deck more clearly now. They were both wearing dark coats, caps, and scarves, hiding most of their features. They looked nervous and wary, holding their rifles close to their chests. Jasper wondered if they were members of the French Resistance, or the Belgian Secret Army, or some other underground group. He hoped they were not German spies, or worse, collaborators.

Jasper and Blejack stood on the deck of their boat, waiting for the men to make the first move. They were also armed, but they kept their weapons concealed under their coats. They did not want to scare off the men or provoke them into a fight. They wanted to see the photographs and verify their authenticity. They wanted to know the truth about the Nazi atrocities and expose them to the world.

"Ahoy there!" one of the men on the trawler shouted, in a thick French accent. "I hear the fish are practically blazing when you pull them from the water here"

"Hotter than Wilfred's love scene," Jasper said, reading the word aloud.

That was the password that they had agreed upon with their contact in London. Wilfred was the name of a famous British poet, who had died in the First World War. Neither of them had any idea if he ever wrote a love scene, but neither would a German spy, they hoped.

The men on the trawler looked at each other and nodded. They seemed to relax a bit and lowered their rifles. They reached into their cabin and brought out a large envelope. It was sealed with wax, and had a red cross stamped on it.

"Here they are," the first man said, holding up the envelope. "The photographs. They are from Auschwitz. I suggest if you don't have to look at them yourselves, don't. You won't be able to get it back out of your heads."

He tossed the envelope to Jasper, who caught it with one hand. He felt the weight of it, and the shape of the photographs inside. The manila paper around them was coated with dread. But Jasper already knew what he would see inside. He had known it for over a decade. The images that Athena had revealed to him never stopped haunting him

He looked at Blejack, who nodded back at him. They both knew they had to be careful. They had to check the photographs for any signs of tampering or forgery. They had to make sure they were not being followed or watched. They had to get back to London as soon as possible and deliver the photographs to their superiors. They had to complete their mission and expose the Nazi crimes. Finally convince the Allies of the horror and reality of the situation and get them to take some kind of action.

The other trawler pulled away into the fog and a small motorboat engine started not far away. Paul's large silhouette came into their view above the shape of the smaller boat. He was holding an Enfield rifle with a scope in one hand, and the till of the engine in the other. These were dangerous times and Jasper's crew were no strangers to them. They always tried to have a backup plan for their backup plan. Tonight, it was Paul.

Jasper and Blejack helped the old quartermaster board and the three of them attached the small boat to lift it out of the water.

"Damn, it is frigid out there tonight, Cappy." Paul pulled his coat tight around his neck.

"Isn't it always, when we hit the water together?" Jasper answered.

"It's been that way for a long time now for us. Can we get this war wrapped up? I am ready to go back to the Caribbean." He went on, knowing that didn't seem likely. There was no end in sight. All he knew was every year, the government would say, 'over by Christmas' and this one was fast approaching. Like the last one came and went.

Jasper shook his head, still reeling in the boat.

"I guess that is why we are out here. By the way, Paul," He made sure he had his attention, "Thanks for covering us tonight. You never know when it is going to count."

"Yeah, no problem, Cappy."

Jasper and Paul reached out and pulled the small skiff in over the deck and Blejack started lowering it while they held it.

Jasper puzzled over why Paul didn't give him his normal reply. He must be really cold, he guessed. Maybe he better get some cabin time.

"Blejack, you want to take the wheel? I have to look at these. You might want to miss them."

"No, I came a long way to get our hands on them. I won't let you carry whatever it is alone." He almost scowled at his cousin's suggestion. "But I will head us that way."

"Paul, same offer. You don't have to see these."

"Yeah, isn't that like the world, just don't look at it and there is nothing there, right. I am with Blejack. We took a lot of risks getting this setup. I might as well put the rot in my head too. Too many have looked the other way already."

Jasper went into the cabin and checked the shades were all closed, then lit up a lamp and sat down. He took his knife and slid it through the edge of the package, opening it at one end. Then he looked at Paul who was standing next to him.

"Better get a chair. I already know what we are going to find, and you will want to be sitting, I promise you."

Paul reached over and slid down a chair next to Jasper and seated himself. Jasper pulled the drawer open and lifted a magnifying glass from its contents. Paul looked around the pale room, all painted in white and scuff marks. Smelling of fish that would never be washed away.

Jasper looked intently at each photo, then set it aside. Paul began to pick them up and look at each one. Both were silent as the minutes passed by. Paul looked at every image, just as Jasper did.

Bodies, naked and starved piled up like cord wood. Men and women, sitting in long rows in the cold winter, no more than skeletons. Crowded into beds stacked three and four bunks tall, with barely room to crawl into. It was death. It was worse than what Odysseus would have seen when he went to Hades.

Jasper immediately got chills remembering the frozen corpses of the north Atlantic, coming to him night after night. Hundreds upon hundreds. Not even that compared to what was before him now.

He finally set the glass down and leaned back in the chair, letting out a long sigh. He thought to himself, "Is this the whole of my destiny? To see the mass death of men and women and children, over and over again?"

Paul stood up and just said, "I need to get some air, Cappy."

Jasper didn't look, just shook his head.

He slid the photos back into the large envelope and put them into the desk drawer. Then went to relieve Blejack.

Paul was looking out over the water from the stern, silent and contemplating what he had seen. He tried to warn him. Paul would digest it and put it in its place in a little while.

"They are in the drawer. I didn't want them flying all over the room with you at the wheel." He nudged Blejack off the ships helm.

"You are lucky you made it out of there alive." He chided the captain right back.

"You really may not want to look at them." Jasper nodded toward Paul.

"It's that bad, is it?"

"Probably worse. I have had years to prepare for it. I just tried to block out the big picture and focus on the grain of the images."

"Jasper, I already told you, I will never let you carry it alone. That is just how it is for us."

Blejack went below and remained there for a good stretch. And he came back as silent as the others. Taking his spot beside the wheel next to the small wall that broke the mist from the captain's stand.

They eased quietly into the cove and slipped the fishing boat up to the dock. The sentry stood back in the shadows of the globes that dimly lit the small pier, but they saw him. They knew the sentry, and he knew them. He was one of their guys. S.I.S. All of the sentries on this small pier were S.I.S.

The three tied off the boat and made the short walk toward him. Behind him were rough steep hills with tiny bits of scrub growing out in patches.

"How did it go tonight?" he asked them.

"Progress I guess," Jasper answered.

There were no secret pass phrases or questions here. Not other than conversation.

"When are you three old farts going to retire?"

"Maybe when all of you young shits stop having wars." Jasper gave him a grin, feeling his win.

Three men in their mid to late sixties, still playing the spy game. They were pretty good at it. Practically in their blood.

"He is waiting for you at the shop." the young sentry informed them. "Said he would stay there until you guys came back in."

"Good, sooner we make this check in the better." Jasper nodded to him and the three of them started walking down the wooden planked walkway.

They all got into Blejack's old Chrysler and shut the doors. Waited to hear the whining grind of his starter forcing the cast iron beast into life. It did not let them down. Jasper thought, another ten minutes and they would even get some heat in the cab.

"Next stop, South Hampton. Blejack will be your conductor and engineer. And the dining car is closed because there isn't one."

"Take us in witch-doctor." Jasper laid his head back on the seat and closed his eyes.

It was going to be a long trip tonight, eighty miles in the fog with black out headlights. Probably sunup before we make it there.

"I don't doubt you for a minute, cousin, but if you get too tired, let me know and I will give you a rest." the captain probably said, not sure as his lights began to dim.

"Yeah, you get your rest, old man. I will have us in the parking lot when you wake."

Blejack looked in the mirror and Paul was already head against the armrest and feet up on the sail panel in the back seat, sawing the logs.

He thought, 'Just like old times, Blejack takes the helm, and they can get their beauty sleep and do their preening when they wake up.' He smiled at his private joke and started slicing away at the miles.

It was dark and the fog gave him just the shortest view ahead. He wasn't crawling along, but it wasn't a full walk for the 38 New York Special either. He barely noticed as he passed the stainless grill on the left of the road until two dots of light appeared behind them.

Blejack rubbed his neck with his right hand and gave it a little twist to get the blood flowing. Only giving the tiny blips in the fog, the slightest attention.

After about a mile it seemed they were keeping pace with him. He relaxed and focused most of his attention ahead. Then he caught a glimpse of a red taillight through the heavy mist in front of them.

He reached up and turned the knob on the headlight switch, dimming the dash. 'Practically rush hour, at three a.m.,' he thought.

The small dots in the rear-view mirror started to grow slightly.

"Crap!" he muttered, "We are going get my Chrysler messed up."

He gently punched Jasper, "Get up old man, we got bad company."

Jasper opened his eyes, "Paul, time to go to work."

Paul rolled over, as though he was going to ignore the call, then reached under the back of the driver's seat and pulled out a small m1 carbine.

Jasper flipped down a door that was built into the base of the front seat below him and pulled out a Thompson.

Both were fairly short for rifles. Maybe three and a half feet long. In fact, the m1 was based on the Thompson. They were light, easy to use and decently reliable.

Magazines clicked and shells chambered.

Paul tapped the back of his seat, "Whenever you are ready, Blejack."

"You boys, try to save my car."

Jasper grinned in the dim light of the dash, "Have we ever let you down?"

"No, not if I don't count the last five of my cars. Paul, don't you damn open that back door either. Wind will tear it off."

"Relax, don't you have some shrunken skull or wad of hair to protect you tonight?" Paul rolled down his windows on both sides in the back.

"I really liked this one." Blejack shook his head, already convinced that it was going to be laid over filled with bullet holes and in flames before the sun came up.

As they were getting prepared for the fight and chase, the car behind them sped up alongside Blejack's Chrysler. The driver didn't even look over.

Both Paul and Jasper sat at the ready to open their cannons on it.

It went on past and crept slowly ahead of them.

"Oh, thank god," Blejack let out.

"See, it is all fine." Jasper smiled.

The taillights of the passing car indicated that it was going around the car that had been in front of them for the last few minutes.

Paul started in on Blejack from the back, "It is a nice car, burgundy paint too. You can't pay enough money now to get burgundy paint."

Blejack rapidly tapped Jasper on the arm. "Bloody hell."

The two cars ahead them were running side by side now. A third car now appeared in the mirror.

"Okay, the problem here is we are going in the wrong direction, Bleej. There are more cars in front of us than there are behind."

"I see what you mean, Jasper. Let's hope that the road is just moist enough."

Blejack pushed on the gas pedal, moving toward the cars in front of them faster. Just before he could see the full outline of the vehicles with his covered headlights, he cranked on the wheel and slammed on the brakes.

The big car tipped its roof and began to spin on its rear tires, and he hit the gas pedal again, giving the car a hard jerk.

He fought the wheel and pulled the sedan back in line and hammered the pedal down to the floor, shooting past the third car that had appeared behind them.

Jasper watched out his window, looking for anything to give them a little edge if the cars turned around behind them.

He gave Blejack a tap on the arm, "There, pull up that hill."

Blejack slowed and turned into the narrow road and killed his lights, easing it up the hill. He shoved it into reverse and shut it off, pulling the parking brake.

Jasper handed him another m1 and the three jumped out of the car and ran the short distance back down the hill.

Paul knelt down by a fence post and Blejack and Jasper ran across the road to the opposite side and crouched down in the fog, spreading out back toward the direction they were going in a moment ago.

They could hear them before they could see them. They had their lights off. That meant they were looking.

Jasper remained still behind a low rock wall, watching the first car pass.

Blejack let it pass too.

The second car came rolling quietly in front of Jasper and then there was the popping of a pair of gunshots.

Both Jasper and Blejack lit up the second and third cars.

Men started jumping from the cars and firing back.

Jasper crouched and ran along behind the short wall, then stuck his head up and eased off a pair of shots. Another man down and he was moving again.

There was a heavy burst of fire back toward Paul as he cleared everyone from the first car. They had gotten out after it had rammed into the ditch when the driver failed to function. They made the mistake of congregating at the rear of the car where they were easy pickings for Paul.

Blejack had moved some stones to give him a good portal to fire though and keep his head protected. He was taking his time, getting a target and then removing it.

It looked like Jasper was the only one having to work for it tonight. His group had spread out on him. But he was down to two. The problem was now, they were both moving in on him at once from either end of the wall. And his magazine was jammed with mud and grass.

He pushed his back into the cold stones and prepared to feel that burning pain that always came with a shell passing through his skin and watched to see which one would come over the wall first.

He rushed to clear the magazine and slot and get it reloaded into the rifle as they both stepped over at once, aiming their guns in his direction, the sound of gunfire went into the air, and Jasper closed his eyes, 'well, here it comes', he thought.

Blejack came walking down from behind him and said, "Well, let's go. We still have an hour of driving, and I didn't get a nap like you."

Jasper grinned and got up from the ground.

They looked the men over, "Know any of them?" Paul asked.

"Nah, no telling. But they don't want us getting to where we are going, do they, Paul," the now wet and dirty captain answered.

"We better clear this road, so we don't have a pile up in the fog." Blejack pointed his thumb at the cars.

"Yeah, let's just run 'em up the shoulders and get going. They can send someone else out here to take care of the rest." Jasper agreed as he slipped behind the wheel of one of the vehicles that were just pursuing them.

They each got one off the road, then hastily dragged the bodies over to the side next to the cars.

Blejack got to his car before the other two and quickly threw down a jacket he had retrieved from the car he had moved on the passenger side seat.

Jasper opened the door and looked at it.

"Don't get that mud in my seats."

Jasper looked at the jacket again, "Well, it has blood on it."

"Don't care. I don't want mud in my seats."

Jasper sat on the blood-spattered jacket, "Fine. Firkin witch-doctor."

Blejack started his beloved 38 Chrysler and rolled back and around, pulling them out onto the road again to resume their journey.

Jasper leaned back, "I knew your car would be fine. Didn't I say that Blejack?"

"No, what you said was, 'have you ever let me down' and that only made me remember the last five cars I had to put to rest. Which if I recall correctly, you also said, 'Have I ever let you down, Blejack,' before they were filled with bullet holes, mud, rolled over, burned and sinking to the bottom of the ocean."

"Oh, yeah, but I never let you down. Look at you. Fit as a fiddle."

"Uh huh, out here, sixty-four years old, meeting the underground at midnight on the channel, fighting spies in the fog, trying to get my car rolled over and punched like a sieve, you have done fine by me."

Jasper could see his grin in the dim light of the dashboard.

"You would prefer getting up at six a.m. and having your crumpets and tea?" Jasper shook his head, saying it as if he was just becoming aware of Blejack's true desire.

"Hell no. We just took down those shits a third our age, supposedly highly trained spies and assassins. And they barely saw what was coming." Blejack still had his m1 sitting next to him and he gave it a soft pat, like he would a small puppy. "Right where I belong."

Jasper laid his head back against the door again, ready to continue his nap. "Take us to port, Blejack"

"Aye, Aye, Cappy."

Chapter 4: Rise!

Lyme Regis, England.
January 23, 1945

ERIN TRIED TO ABSORB the long and unbelievable story the old man had been telling as she walked with her two young boys away from her parent's graves. They were buried only a day after the blast in London that took them from her. The director had told her there was just not enough left for her to look at. And what there was, she wouldn't want to see.

She was carrying the blue flag and the book the man had given to her. Paul said it was Joey, but it had been so long since she had seen him. And he just didn't look that much like Joey. Everything was just so mixed up. And it was all happening so fast.

It was late afternoon now, as the young red-haired woman stepped her way down the cobblestone walks toward the home her parents had raised her in. It would be hers now. For her and the boys, Jim and Joe. They had been living there since she got the news about her husband anyways. Frank was a good man. He was firmly set in his ways, and hard to debate anything with, but he was solid and honest. Sadly, he was also a bomber pilot.

She recalled her father and Frank in the small dining room at this same house. Jasper almost begged her husband not to sign on. That there was a better way to fight this war. He would get him into the SIS with the others and do some real good.

Erin didn't know how to feel about it. It seemed either choice was risky. Frank knew what he was doing when it came to airplanes, but her dad, no one knew war like her dad. He had been behind closed doors through two of them since she was born.

She walked into the small stucco home and found the Chapman's were already there. Wendy was cooking in the kitchen, given away by the scent that filled the house. She could see Craig at the table through the doorway.

The boys rushed in and ran to their room, Erin walked through the arched opening into the kitchen and bent to give him a hug.

"Hi Grampy."

Craig hugged her back, "We are so heartbroken for you, Erin. There is no one else like your parents."

"Thank you." She closed her eyes, checking to see if there were any tears left. Trying to hold them a little while longer so the pain would remain inside like a piece of them, still with her.

Wendy moved away from the cooking and took Erin by the shoulders, "You just sit down right there, I will take care of everything. Just relax and we will all sit and keep each other together tonight."

Erin sat down next to Craig and the old man she got to know as Grampy since she could remember put his arm around her shoulder and held her.

She rested her head on his shoulder for several minutes before remembering what the man said.

"It's all in there, boys. Make sure she reads the book, and right away. She is going to love the ending."

She looked at the rough looking leather-bound book on the table, then picked it up. She sat up and started flipping through the pages. She wasn't the type that liked to skip to the end of book, but something about how he had said it.

The last page had a poem of sorts. And it was dedicated to her by her parents. It was short, and it wasn't that great. No hidden meaning. No duality of perspective to make you think about what you were reading. It was nice. It showed how much her parents had loved each other and how they loved this ship, the Salamander. But where was the thing Joey was talking about? What was it she was going to love in the ending?

TO OUR LITTLE GODDESS, Erin,

We looked at each other and found love.
We looked at the sun and found hope.

We looked at the Salamander and found pride.
We looked at the crew and found a family.
We looked at Erin and found a home.
We sailed the Salamander, and we have lived.

She remembered something her dad had asked her when she was reading a poem from some book to him, "If it doesn't rhyme, is it really a poem?"

Her eyes caught on the last line. "And we have lived."

She started looking closely at the binding sheet on the back cover, just a piece of paper that had been wrapped around the pages when the book was bound. It was glued onto the paperboard and over the thin leather wrapping on the cover so it would be less likely to peel away.

At the bottom corner she could feel an outline on the paper with her thump. There was a Salamander with a few stars around it, and a small lump of something beneath it.

She took a bread knife from the table and started to work it under the edge and peel away the paper from the cover. Below was a tiny note. "Erin, January 23, midnight." and an address.

She thought about it, "What does this mean?" but this was just the kind of thing that she was used to seeing. Codes and hidden messages.

"Grampy, Grammy? Can I ask you a huge favor?" She was still studying the tiny page and the poem.

"Anything, sweetie." Wendy answered.

"Can you keep the boys with you? I think I have something important I need to take care of."

Craig pulled his arm tight on her shoulder, "Of course. As long as you need. We will be here for them."

"You two are priceless to me." She smiled. "I'm sorry, I don't know how long this will take. So, if you need to take them to your house, I will know where to come."

"Not a problem, we have plenty of room for them." Wendy answered.

Wendy turned around and said as if she knew what the note had said, "Go now and take our car. Or you are going to be late."

Erin gave her a puzzled look.

"Erin, get up. The keys are there on the table." Wendy turned back to her cooking.

Craig reached into his pocket and held out something to her, "Here, you had better have this too. One of the boys dropped it by. Your dad would want you to have it. He said you loved it nearly as much as he did."

She held out her hand and the heavy gold watch fell into her palm. She smiled as a hundred memories flashed through her mind.

She got up and set the book down, taking the keys. She grabbed a jacket from the hooks on the wall and went out to take their car. It was a long drive to Liverpool. Wendy was right whether she knew where Erin had to go or not. If she didn't put her foot down, she wasn't going to make it.

Erin waved at the boys through the window as she slipped into the Jaguar sedan. The Chapman's had some pretty good connections. Craig had been the one who got her father involved with government intelligence years and years ago. It was rare to have a good car in England, even more rare one that could do 95 miles per hour.

She tore through the miles to Liverpool, not slowing until she saw the first buildings of the city. It was well into the night by then. She was only a dozen blocks from the address when the car started to make a clunking sound and steam began to pour out from the front of the bonnet.

She looked at the clock on the dash and pulled the dying car to the curb. She could still make it on foot.

As she gathered her jacket and her dad's watch from the passenger seat she noticed another car, back behind her. It had pulled off to the side too. It was about a half a block back and she could see the outline of at least two men inside.

She struggled to get the jacket on inside the small cab and slipped the pocket watch into its pocket.

She pretended to adjust her make up and studied the men in the car. They were just sitting there. She had been followed.

She was now angry with herself. How could she be so stupid? She let her guard down. She had lost herself in her grief and focused on figuring out what would be waiting for her at the end of this trip, and she had made mistakes.

Well, there was nothing to do now. The car was done. It would take an hour for it to cool off enough to start and she didn't have time to lose them on the streets if it did start.

She got out and started walking away, forward. Listening.

She heard the quiet creaks of their doors. The soft tap of shoes touching the street.

She started to look for an escape. Anything. She had to get loose from these guys and get to that address.

They were trying to walk quietly, but she heard every step like the pounding of a drum.

She tried to meter her own walk. Not give away that she knew they were there.

She stepped past a small store and saw their reflection in the angled glass of the doorway. Four men in dark coats and hats. Not the friendly looking types.

At the end of the store, she bolted to the right down an alley, and burst into a full run.

Then a left, she ran as hard as her legs would carry her.

She could hear them running now behind her and talking or half yelling at each other.

Another left, and she spotted a half torn down building. She quickly hopped over the remnants of a brick wall and ran as softly as she could to the rear, hiding behind another section of wall.

The voices were not far from her now. Probably back at the last corner she had taken. They were deciding which way she went.

She could hear the footsteps begin again. Now some were getting quieter, but some were getting louder.

A man stopped at the front of the broken building she was hiding in. He had on a low brimmed hat and a cigarette in his mouth. He stood there, lighting it and she could almost make out his face.

She pulled herself back behind the wall, depending on her ears now.

The tap and crunch of the steps told her he was now inside the wreckage.

The man was walking slowly and methodically. Coming closer, stopping, the sound of a shoe sliding, grinding against broken brick dust and wood splinters.

Then she could hear his breath. Right beside her head.

Before he could inhale again, she pounced on him like a cat trapped in a corner.

She threw one arm around his neck then the other locked behind his head, and she threw her full weight into the air, nearly running against the wall, twisting his head and body until she heard a snap.

She landed on her feet and looked down at the lump of dark cloth on the ground.

A quick glance out into the street, and she knelt down to get a look at who it was that had been after her. No surprise that she didn't recognize him.

She dug through his pockets, looking for anything. Identification, letters, anything that could give her a clue.

She found a few things and shoved them into her pockets. No time, not now.

She quickly walked to the side of the building and climbed up onto an old shelf and over the eight feet of wall that was still there.

She looked at her watch and took in where she was, getting her bearings, she pulled off her shoes and began running again.

She ran down several streets, turned corners and then finally passed under a streetlight, and across the roadway, she rushed into a darkened doorway. She could still hear the muffled voices in the dark behind where she had come from. She slowly inched her eyes around the corner of the wall to see if they were there.

Pulling back, she looked at the number on the small, covered entry. She bent her head down to look at the small piece of paper again and make sure this was the place.

Erin heard the door open, but the man's hand was over her mouth and pulling her backwards before she could react.

She struggled to break free as the door shut behind her.

The man pulled away his hand and turned her around by her shoulder.

She stood in shock, frozen.

Her life was in subterfuge. Working in the shadows. Gathering information, seeing what very few others ever saw. But this was beyond anything else. This was impossible.

Tears started to flow from her eyes as she became aware of what was in front of her.

The man who had pulled her into the room put his arms around her nearly taking her breath away and then another pair wrapped around her waist, squeezing her.

She couldn't fight them or make sense of this. She couldn't pull away from them. She began to sob uncontrollably.

The young man and woman with red hair and blue eyes were her parents. Her parents, but thirty years younger. And alive.

They let her go from their grip and a third woman stepped up to her. This one had red hair and blue eyes too, but she was wearing a white dress, almost a gown, strapped at the waist with a gold and silver belt.

Her beauty was incredible. Maybe more beautiful than her own mother.

She knelt before Erin and wrapped a broad belt around her waist, and yet another ginger haired woman, dressed much the same, handed her a round gold talisman, it was about three inches around and was shaped like a flattened orb. It was hollow with ribbons of gold making the shapes of the continents. Small gold shapes were locked inside. A heart, an apple and a trident.

The woman placed the talisman onto the belt like a large buckle, then looked into her eyes as she took her hand and placed her palm onto the front of it.

Like watching a plant germinate, gold and silver armor began to grow out around her body. Armlets and leggings, breast plate, a heavy gold necklace and almost a crown. It was carved and had shapes and runes like you might see in a mythological painting.

She stood up and placed both of her hands on the sides of Erin's head, then without moving her lips, Erin heard a whisper inside.

"Erin Rise."

SHE FELT A TINGLING at first then her eyes began to glow. Something somewhere between tortuous pain and ecstasy filled her body as blue electric flames began to crawl across her skin.

She turned her head up and her mouth dropped open. The look of rage or the pain of death was on her face.

Something like lightning roared out onto her arms and around her body.

It broke through her skin like cracks in porcelain.

"It is part of you Erin. Don't fight it. Hold it. Hold it like you hold one of your boys."

Erin began to scream as the power overcame her. She thrust her arms out wide, and her feet left the floor as she bent backwards.

"Erin, hold onto it. You can control it. You have before." The woman told her softly, speaking into her mind.

Maeve and Jasper watched, helpless to shield their baby this time. She would make it. She would find her way through the awakening.

"Erin, it is the warm blanket that saved you from the sea. Pull it close around you. Let it protect you."

The other two women stepped forward now, holding out their hands a large ball of light and sparks surrounded Erin and Aphrodite. Containing the power that was sleeping inside this young woman.

Aphrodite started to tell Erin her story. All directly into her mind. She showed her who she was. The daughter of Maeve, the granddaughter of Aphrodite who had to be hidden and protected since she was born. But now it was time to wake up. It was time to go to work. It was time to save the world, and it was time to Rise.

Erin burst out into blue fire and electricity. The globe that Eris and Athena held around them surged and flickered. Aphrodite stood there before Erin inside the protective shield, with the blue flames held only inches away from her body.

"Erin, hold onto it. Don't be afraid of it. This is always who you were."

Erin's eyes started to cool from the bright blue torches and back to her naturally radiant blue.

"Yes, you are doing good. There you go. Pull it back into yourself."

Erin began to hold back the eruption, slowly receding to her arms then her hands until it finally went out in a small flicker of light and a dull glow in her palms.

Her new acquaintance took a step and pulled Erin into her arms as she went almost limp. She laid her head on the woman's shoulder, exhausted, mentally, and physically.

Jasper broke the silence.

"We thought it was time that you met the rest of your family, sugar. I am sorry we could not do it more gradually. But we are up against the clock."

Erin did not move. She was looking around the room. Blejack, not dead. Joey, not old. Paul, not old. Her parents are not dead and not old. And we have the Grecian trio here. All seemed ready and dressed for the toga party. She noted the other two more prepared to be the sentries or guards at said party. They were armored just as she was now. And both had weapons.

But not this woman who held her. Her mind raced trying to put all the pieces where they should go.

Jasper continued. "So, this would be your grandmother, who is holding you. Her name is Aphrodite. You may have heard stories about her. And over there, the one that looks like she is the cat that ate the mouse, that is your aunt, Eris. The other one with the more serious demeanor, your great aunt, Athena."

Eris looked at the two women, still scrambling inside for a rational explanation.

"Now, if you think all of that is impossible, I need you to remember what just happened and that your 'not dead' father is telling you this. And he isn't sixty-seven years old."

Erin got control of herself and lifted her cheek from who was apparently the new grammy. As she stood up straight, the woman looked into her eyes.

"Don't worry. You have seen my face many times, and you will remember. You have had enough tonight though. We would normally do this sort of thing far from the mortal world. But like your dad said, there is a clock ticking."

Erin looked at Maeve. She only imagined what her mother looked like when she was her age. Her dad used to tell her, a goddess on earth.

Maeve smiled and grabbed Erin in her arms. "My baby, I am so sorry we hurt you. We had to do it this way. Our enemies needed to believe we were dead. And our enemies are much more powerful than the feeble headed Nazis."

Athena spoke up from by the large bulletin board, "Take a few minutes, Maeve, you three, then we need to get started. We can't wait any longer. We start tonight. And I am sorry Erin, that will mean you too. It will mean millions of lives what we begin here in this room. So, look around at the people you know and trust, and believe that they would point you in the right direction."

Erin looked at the woman, curious and concerned. What about her own children? What were they getting her into? What in heaven's name did her body just do?

Athena acted as though she could see Erin's thoughts. "There is more than one reason you have been watched over and protected since before your birth, young Erin. In all of the men and gods before, you were the only one ever granted the power of Zeus himself. And, well, you are family." She gave Aphrodite a roll of her eyes.

Her stepsister smiled back at her with a bit of a gleam in her own. Over two thousand years the two half siblings had squabbled, until Maeve and Jasper, and then baby Erin. And their father had decided to finally not just sit on the fence and watch everything unfold. He had chosen a side and had let them have free reign to finish it.

Three of the women who were instrumental in the beginning of the Trojan war would be the end of this one. And they would be on the same side.

Only one God stood outside of the fold. One whose jealous rage had reached over centuries and decades. Who started war after war and walked among men, influencing their thoughts, technology and weapons. Whose anger over the love that gave birth to Erin's mother, Maeve could not be sated.

His deception leading Maeve and Jasper into a bomb target set everything into motion that Erin was seeing now. Zeus, seeing Ares had broken the agreement, set aside the rules. The clock was turned back for her parents and their friends.

Only Uncle John was not there. He chose not to give up the rest of his life with his wife and children and grandchildren. He would face death when it came for him. But he would help in any other way.

Erin had absorbed all she could. She just held her parents in disbelief.

They lifted her to her feet and her dad said, "Erin, this is going to be bad, but it is what we are up against. And we have no time. We must act now, or all of them will die."

Erin stepped to the long table in front of the bulletin board with the large map, lines and pins and marks on it. Before her were the photos. Hundreds. And drawings. And names. And it was horrible. Just eyes looking out from skeletons. Barbed wire and evil men in black uniforms with their smug confidence.

Her eyes began to glow again.

Maeve and Aphrodite both put a hand on each shoulder.

"Hold it back." Aphrodite spoke to her in her mind.

Erin closed then opened her eyes again. She looked at her mother with tears.

"I know, it is hard. Millions have already been lost. We cannot keep you hidden anymore, at least not your power. We are going over the channel and we are going to turn the war upside down and put an end to it."

Erin looked at the other women, the goddesses, "Can't you just stop them?"

Eris grinned, "I could."

Athena gave her a sharp glance, "No. We cannot just stop it. We must make men think that they stopped it. Or tomorrow, we will be watching the next war, even worse than this one. They must see the horrors that they create. They must suffer the loss and the guilt of their actions. They must choose their destiny. But we are going to help them move along a little faster. And we are going to balance things out a little bit."

"So, it's complicated?" Erin remarked, having heard that line many times.

"Yeah, it's complicated." Athena smiled. Recognizing the touch of defiance in her tone. "Someone has a little of her father inside there too. I like it."

Paul, Blejack and Joey all gathered around the table with the others, and they began to plan and give assignments. Aphrodite and Athena would go to the Allied command and put some ideas into their minds. Eris would do what she enjoyed. She would go to the camp these images were taken at and throw a monkey wrench into things. Erin would go with Eris. It would be a baptism in fire for her, but there was no one more powerful than Eris on a battlefield. Erin would be safe and start to adjust to her powers.

Maeve was drowning in concern for her daughter, but Aphrodite and Eris both insisted. She is strong enough. And she will see first-hand why she will need to do the things she will do afterward. Maeve and Jasper and the three men would be scattered out, working within the underground and intelligence communities. Then when the camps in the east were resolved, they would begin to reunite.

Maeve couldn't understand why they wouldn't let her go with Erin. She pleaded with Aphrodite.

"Sweet daughter, you have spent your life patching up wounded soldiers and men and women. If you went with them on this mission, you would get personally involved. It would tear into your soul in a way that you could never repair it. It would put you at risk and Erin, and the mission. You have to trust us on this. We haven't been protecting her this long to let her be harmed. And Eris could smile and kiss her fingertip and wipe out everyone inside of a hundred miles. She will be safe."

Fifteen minutes later it seemed like everyone knew where they were going, except Joey.

"Uh, guys? What do you need me to do?"

Eris grinned, "Joey, we are going to need a driver. We have a few stops to make on the way."

Joey wasn't sure he liked the look of her grin. But he was glad to be with Erin. One of the crew needed to keep an eye on their baby girl.

Chapter 5: Sisters of Chaos

Auschwitz, Poland.
January 27, 1945

ERIS TOOK HER YOUNG niece's hand, "Erin, what you are going to see here today, some of the brightest military and government minds in the world have found a way to turn their eyes from."

Erin was not on her feet. She had been jerked out of reality four days ago. She saw the pictures. But pictures never show you what is on the outside of the box. She knew this was going to be bad.

"We are going to stop that today. I am going to take you inside, and they won't be able to see either of us. You have to be quiet. I won't keep you inside long. But you have to see. Then I will go do what has to be done here."

Erin looked at Eris, three days together, and she still couldn't figure this one out. She did resemble herself, and she had nice armor too. There was something very dark and deadly about her though. Just hiding beyond that overly charming grin she liked to wear in the most inappropriate moments.

"Just keep holding my hand, Erin. And I will have you out of there in minutes. Whatever you do, don't let yourself power up. You will break my shielding and expose us both."

"Let's go, waiting doesn't make it easier." Erin grits her teeth slightly.

Then they are inside the fences. Eris shows her the people in the yard. Freezing in the cold January winds. Then she takes her inside the barracks. Bunks, two and three people laying on hard wooden planks, barely anything but skin and bone, struggling to keep each other warm.

The room smelled of death and human refuse. Erin's eyes burned and she tried to compartmentalize what she saw. She focused on the big picture, remembering her new sister's warning.

And she saw children. Small girls and boys. Sometimes clinging to a dying mother or father or sister or uncle.

A guard was walking down the passage in the center of one of the barracks and Eris stopped, inches in front of the man. Erin looked into his face, burning its shape into her memory.

She felt Eris squeeze her hand and they were outside again. Looking at a building with tall smokestacks made of brick. She took her to the window and saw the room inside. It was empty except for a few of the prisoners mopping inside.

And then they were inside again. There was a wall that had a row of iron doors, like fireplaces. You could hear the flames inside. It was the sound of a strong wind. A German soldier in a black uniform turned a valve and opened one of the doors, taking a shovel he scraped out ash and bits of bone into a wheel barrel.

Then he walked to the end of the room and yelled something in German. A prisoner came in from a hallway who Erin had just seen in the other room mopping.

The Nazi yelled at the man for a few minutes, pointing back at the wheel barrel he had just been filling. He smacked the man in the head, then shoved him. The broken soul went to the wheel barrel and hoisted it up and began pushing it toward the end of the room and out the door.

Eris made all of the doors transparent so that Erin could see inside. Burning skeletons. Then she took her outside where the man was going with the wheel barrel.

Mounds of ash and trucks were being loaded with it. Eris pointed outside the area where the trucks were. And she exposed what was inside the earth. More bodies, all stripped of their flesh. Some burnt. Some just decayed. Hundreds upon hundreds.

Eris felt the tingle in Erin's hand and transported them into a forest.

She released Erin, and the lights began. Like inside the room just a few nights ago. But this time, Aphrodite wasn't there to talk her through it.

ERIN'S BODY WAS COVERED with runes written in blue light. Her eyes blazed blue again and her arms were covered with power like an electrical transformer in a thunderstorm.

She opened her mouth in a silent scream and the blue light flared from within her.

Eris watched her younger sister's daughter in awe. There was no question why Zeus would never have given this power to her. She would have blazed across the earth.

Just when it seemed like Erin's body might erupt there on the spot and take the earth with her, Eris got a shock. Not from her electrical outbreak.

It was as if the power suddenly found its center and it pulled back into Erin. Light began to form behind her, spreading out in the shape of wings. Broad feathered wings like an eagle. But she didn't look like your average angel. If she were an angel in that moment, she was the angel of death.

"Well, this is new." Eris said smiling a genuine smile this time. By genuine, I mean not the creepy one she uses when she is about to snap someone's neck.

Eris drew a circle around Erin with her finger in the air.

"Are you back with me, Erin?"

Erin stood there, looking into space. Not saying anything.

"Erin, snap out of it. I need you here."

Erin turned her still glowing eyes toward Eris.

"Okay, shut that off. You are starting to give me the jitters, and that is not something I am used to."

Erin brought herself back down, and her eyes cleared. This time she didn't collapse, there were no tears. There was cold purpose in her eyes.

"Good, we are getting someplace now. Now you will be ready. You stay right here. Right in that spot. I have a blind around you. No one can see you or hear you, not even a god. I have some work to do back there. Something I am well suited for. When I get back, then you will see what you are suited for."

Erin still didn't mutter a word.

"Erin, are we good to go? I need you all here for this. What you saw in there, that is just one place, just the surface. And today, you and I, we are not going to let them get away with it."

"Okay. I will be ready. Whatever it is you do, you do it like you never have before."

Eris lit up like a candle. She even gave Erin a little kiss on the cheek. "Oh, you are truly a woman after my own heart. I will indeed do my best work today."

She stepped back, "Remember, stay here. I will only be a few minutes."

Erin sat down and crossed her legs, looking at her hands.

"Just a few minutes, Erin. I will be right back."

ERIS RUSHED BACK INTO the camp and saw several guards leading more of their prisoners toward the extermination chamber.

They must already know, she thought. The Russian soldiers are only 20 or 30 miles away. And now they want to kill as many as they can before making their escape.

She went to work right there. Whispering to each man that they had to go, they had to leave now, or they would be left behind to take the blame. She told them to ask the other guard. He would say the same thing.

And so, they did. They started talking to each other in German and then they were walking away from their prisoners toward the gate.

Then she went to the guard at the gate and told him that these men were trying to desert. Don't believe anything they say. They are going to get everyone caught.

Within seconds the guards were all arguing at the gate.

She saw the commandant step out of his office and she soared next to him. "You need to bring order to your troops. But you have lost your voice, and you can't write."

She went on, guard to guard, giving them opposing orders, causing them to countermand each other and send other guards to do idiotic things. The whole camp was in disarray.

Some men were shot trying to desert. Others were blocking doors so no one could get into the offices or even the barracks.

When she felt satisfied with her work, she returned to the forest where Erin would be waiting.

WHILE ERIS WAS GONE, Erin had stood up and let her power flow again. She threw bolts of blue lighting hitting trees, cutting them in half, then using her energy, she learned she could grab them as they fell and make them fall where she wanted.

Blue fireball after blue fireball, each one coming faster than the last, soon she was flying above the spot she was sitting in before and cutting down a clearing in the forest around her.

The rage inside her was boiling over.

She had her arms spread wide open and was leaning back looking into the sky when Eris popped up next to her, floating beside her.

"Well, you did stay inside the circle, I guess. Are you feeling better?"

"Yes, I think I am. Now, what am I here for?" Erin felt like she was now finding her feet beneath her, albeit a good distance from the ground.

"Well, let's get you back down below the trees before anyone sees you first." Eris tipped her head back toward the ground.

"Take my hand, we will go get you busy."

Erin held out her hand without any hesitation this time.

They appeared on the edge of a wood, next to a rail line. She saw a train coming down the track with smoke billowing up into the air.

"They are bringing more people, Erin. You are going to stop that engine without blowing it off the tracks. Just focus on the engine itself. You can melt it inside and lock it up. Focus and control it little sis. We want to save those people too."

"You know you're my aunt, right?" Erin asks her.

"Well, that is kind of a mortal thing. I just like you, and sisters are closer than aunts and nieces, aren't they?"

"Well, if you say so. But I don't know if that is really true, sis."

Erin burst out her wings and flew directly at the engine coming toward her. Her eyes lit up and blue flames shot from her hands. Seconds later the sound of breaking steel and the wheels locking up and squealing down the top of the tracks.

The engineer and a nazi guard jumped from the engine and tried to run away from her, terrified. Erin didn't blink, she hit them both and they burned to dust.

Eris appeared at her side, "There are more guards. Do you want them to escape here today and disappear into the world, never being known for who they are? Or do you want us to correct that right now?"

Erin looked over at her, "Where are they?"

"Come on, I will show you."

HER FIRST DAY ON THE job and Erin was showing some potential. There were no guards leaving that train today.

Then Eris took her to another place. Miles away from the camp, Nazi soldiers were in a small town, holding guns on people and taking their clothes. Trying to disguise themselves.

"Just wait. It is almost time." Eris whispered.

The men jumped back into their vehicles with their spoils and started leaving the town. Eris and Erin followed them.

"Erin, focus on all of the cars. Stop their engines."

"At once?"

"Yes. At once. You aren't used to it, but you can do it."

Erin looked at the cars speeding away down the road and focused as Eris had told her to.

There was a piercing high-pitched sound and dozens of lines of blue fire shot from her hands. All of the cars stopped.

"Erin, these men are leaving that camp. They were in charge and now they are planning to escape while the men left behind hide the evidence of their crimes. How do we judge them?"

"Eris, you will soon stop asking me that question."

Erin's wings spread out wide and she dived down onto the stalled cars. Men were out and running away from their broken machines. She flew past them then turned and floated to the ground in front of them. She wanted them to see her. See their judgment.

She walked toward them, fierce anger in her eyes. One at a time, balls of blue ripped from her palms, tearing through flesh and bone. The smell of burned flesh matching the smell that these men had grown love so much.

Men tried to run, and she reached her ropes of current around them, dragging them screaming back to her. Looking them in the eyes as she cut them in half.

Another man hiding under a car, and she walked over, opening a gas can on the back of it, then the cap on the fuel tank. Touched the car with her finger, like dialing a phone, and it burst into flames. She stepped away and it exploded behind her.

Eris watched her. She watched the cold determination on her sister's baby's face. There was no joy, no happiness in what Erin was doing. She was judgment. And that is what Eris needed to know. She didn't need any competition after all. And she was supposed to protect Erin, inside and out.

Eris decided that Erin was going to be fine. She was getting a handle on her powers, and she wasn't corrupted. Not even in her present company.

All of them needed to know that Erin was going to handle this. That she would be able to ascend to her position and not turn evil or be devoured by emotions and thoughts that would make things worse.

Eris flew in next to Erin and gave her another rare Eris treat, a gentle smile.

"Okay, I will help you clean this up, and we have a few more stops to make today. I will help with the rest so we can get done and out of here."

Eris dropped to the ground, and she walked swinging her hips like she was in a night club. Pointing to one man's body after another, they turned to dust floating off into the wind. Then she torched each of the cars, leaving them burning and smoking and she jumped back into the air beside Erin.

"Let's go," she said casually and grabbed Erin by the hand.

They were back at the camp, the last of the guards were trying to race away from the gates, locking it behind them.

The prisoners just stood watching. Not knowing what was coming next.

Eris whispered, "I slowed them down. Chaos is what I do."

She winked at Erin, and they were above a sedan racing down a dirt road away from the camp.

"Time for some fun, sis." Eris smiled and the front tire on the car burst. Flapping and wobbling the car ground to a halt.

The voices of the men in the car yelling at each other came from below.

"What do you say we just go down there and beat their asses. You know, like a girl's night. Two sisters, just hanging out." Eris gives her trademark grin.

Erin smiled back, a little uncomfortably, "Normally I would pass, but it is kind of a special occasion, isn't it. The new sisterhood and all."

Eris shook her head in agreement.

They both landed hard behind the car. Walking slowly toward the men who had gotten out of the front seat, now at the rear of the car, getting tools out of the trunk.

They both looked up, stunned and stupid in their black ss uniforms. Eris drew back a fist and clocked the first in the side of his head and he fell to his knees.

"Awe, that was too hard, I was trying for softer."

Erin put her fist into the other's chest.

"Do I hit harder too?" she asked as the man sailed through the air and hit the back of the car.

"Hard to say, I never felt you hit before. Try another and see how it comes out."

They took turns using the two as punching bags and trading comments with each other while the men in the back seat sat and watched with their mouths open.

"I think this one is broken, Erin. Not superior grade race genetics."

She dropped the man, wheezing and bleeding from his mouth and ears.

Erin hit her pin cushion once more, "This one is kind of soft. I can't tell if anything is breaking when I hit it."

Eris just shook her head. "I am disappointed. But there are officers inside the car. Certainly, they would be the best grade that the Nazis have to offer."

Erin kicked the man in the head that she had dropped a moment ago.

"I bet you are right. We just need to move up the chain of command."

They both walked up beside the back doors and looked in with grins at the two officers, now holding pistols pointed at them.

"Really? The superior race and you aren't up for a little hand to hand combat?" Erin asks them.

She focused on both Lugers and turned them red hot.

The men dropped them to the floor as both exploded, sending shrapnel through the seat and floor.

"Now, let's get you boys out of there. It seems too dangerous with all the exploding going on." Eris opened the door, and Erin, not being one to stand on the side, helped her new friend out of the car as well.

Erin aimed her punches into the officer's chest, breaking ribs and cartilage.

"Do you like poetry, Eris?"

"I do," she moved her head side to side, studying her work on the man's face, "But not that stuff that doesn't rhyme."

"I know," Erin hits the man a little lower, not wanting to turn his lights off just yet, "Is that even poetry?"

"I don't think it is. And I have had some poetry written about me. I am practically an authority on the stuff."

"Thank you. Even my dad doesn't think it is poetry." Erin sees the man's eyes start to shut and slaps his face a few times.

"I always liked your dad. He is a smart man. And I like he took good care of you, even for a mortal. He did good."

"I think that other one is still breathing, how are yours?" Erin switched topics again.

"I think there is just enough left for us to have a little talk with them."

"Oh, that is perfect, let's have a talk with them." Erin answers back like a giddy school kid.

Eris drags the second of her catch to the back of the car and sits him down like a rag doll next to the first.

Erin does the same, now all four of them leaning against the bumper, choking and gasping in their own blood.

"You see guys, we know what you did. And if we had time, we would take the next five years or so to give you every bit the same treatment. But we have a time crunch. You can see our problem here. I bet you thought the same thing just a few minutes before we dropped in. So, we have to give you the compressed version."

One of the men was trying to speak. Eris rolled her eyes, annoyed.

"Okay, I was in the middle of a nice speech here, I have been preparing it for minutes, but if you think you have something more important to say, go ahead."

With blood and foam coming from his mouth, he managed to get out a question.

Are you Angels or Demons?

"Oh, how cute. Angels or Demons, he asks." Eris burst into orange and red flames, Erin taking a cue lit herself up in glowing blue.

"I am a goddess, and she is judgment. We find you guilty. You will not even enter Hades. Your thousand years ends here, tonight. And in just a couple of months, your fearless leader will shoot himself in the head like the coward he always was."

With that she made all four men burn slowly from their feet first, feeling the pain and fire, screaming as it climbed to their hearts and then they were dust.

Eris lit their car on fire, which seemed to be a thing with her, then she turned to Erin.

"Assholes."

Erin started to laugh, and Eris grabbed her hand again and they were gone.

This time they were outside a town near the camp. Oswiecim. A large group of SS soldiers were marching down a road by a field.

"Just crush them and I will bury them here." Eris says to her. "Focus your thoughts on their hearts and lungs. If a few of them burn up, it will be fine. But leave some for me to bury. Remember, what we do out here has repercussions across time."

She watches as Erin begins to concentrate. Her eyes were glowing, but she wasn't unleashing the flame.

Eris looks below as men begin to fall and collapse.

"Very good, Eris. You are learning fast."

And then a man burst into flames, and another.

"Okay, well, it is your first day."

"No, I did that on purpose. I remember their faces from the camp." Erin jerked her hands in front of her and the rest of the column fell to their faces.

Eris makes a mark in the air with her finger and the ground opens up, pulling away from the corpses and they tumble and slide into the ground, several feet below. She seems to release her hold and the earth closes up over their bodies.

"Okay, Erin, I think it is time we got you out of here. I am not the best influence, you know. But I think you will do fine."

"So, this was all some sort of test?" Erin asked, somewhat irritated.

"In a way it was, but a test you gave yourself. I just brought you here and showed you what you needed to see." Eris held her hand out to Erin, "Let me take us away from here and we will talk before we go back to the others."

Erin took her hand and a second later they were in the lagoon on the beach in Brazil.

"I loved this place." Eris looked out at the trees and quiet waters. "I came here often while you were a baby. Even before that. I watched over your mom for years. Her whole life really."

Erin looked out onto the waters and remembered the eel.

"Erin, I was just a safety valve for you. If something went wrong, if you couldn't control your power, I would have put you inside a bubble, like Athena and I did a few nights ago. Do you understand?"

"I am getting there. Go on."

"Well, I had to take you without the others, especially your mom. She would have gotten protective and held you back. We needed you to release everything and still have it under your own control. When I took you out of the camp into the woods, you did it. If you hadn't found your center, you could have blown a hole through the entire planet. And that is why I was there for you. Athena is too forceful. Aphrodite is too soft. No one else could have been able to help you."

Erin's eyes showed that she was starting to understand.

"You were a walking bomb. Once you were awoken, you needed to be able to find that control, away from the people you love. People you could have hurt. And you needed just the right person, in this case, goddess, to help you light the fire. But I was also the right person to help you release it."

Erin turned her face down and let out a little laugh.

"She will give me hell about that little altercation at the car. Maybe we can skip that one in the debriefing."

"Honestly, Eris, oh my god I needed to do that."

"Aunties are the best, huh?"

"Hell yeah."

"Okay, I am not out here trying to create a serial killer, so, let's take you back to your mom and dad and now, you are ready. You know your power and you can handle it, and, best of all, you are a good person, Erin."

"Wait, ready for what?"

"Well, to go on your own. You might get some surprises. Like the wings, I wasn't expecting that. But you can handle it. You did an amazing job today. You mastered multi lines of focus, that little thing with the trees, that was cool, tossing them around. You are ready for whatever comes at you."

"On my own?"

"Not always, and you can call on me or any of us if you need us. But we are going to get busy. It is coming fast, and we don't have much time. We aren't just ending this war. We are preventing the next one. If we don't stop that one, the world burns."

"Wait, what?"

"Nope, no more questions. It's time to go." Eris holds her hand out to her young niece.

Chapter 6: Number Two Whitehall Court

SIS Headquarters, London, England.
January 29, 1945

ERIN WALKS DOWN THE street, littered with cars, coming and going. People finding their way to work. The tall brick building with columns and domes looms ahead of her. The large arched doorway was like a cave hiding its secrets.

Plumes of fog drifted into the air from cars and trucks, sitting idling. Waiting for their instructions. That is how she felt now. She was parked and left running. Waiting to be told how she was going to make a difference.

The ice and snow crunched under her feet as she kept walking along. Getting the occasional greeting as she passed another face or another hat and scarf. She was back in her tame dress and long thick coat, with her talisman hidden well beneath. And her thoughts gently wove together the images of the last few days.

This morning, she wasn't thinking of the night in Liverpool, but she felt the papers in her pocket from the man who had hunted her that night. She wasn't thinking of her parents or the impossible things in that room or the day she spent in Poland with her crazy aunt.

Erin was thinking of Jimmy and Joe. She spent the day with them yesterday and she didn't know how she was going to reveal to them that their grandparents were still alive, and they were younger, and their mom was some kind of crazy Nazi killing supernatural being.

Going through the tall doors, she checked in with the sentries and showed her identification. They passed her through with no problem. Her job at the SIS now became so much clearer. Things that had been buried or erased were now in the forefront of her mind. The allies had known about these camps for months, maybe longer. But that information never passed her desk and she never heard anyone talk about it.

So, what else were they hiding?

She walked through a long corridor, lined with portraits of past and present SIS directors and agents. Some of them looked stern and serious, others smiled and winked. She wondered, 'what else did they know?' How many soldiers marched right to their own deaths because these brilliant men thought it was strategically important?

She reached the end of the corridor and entered a large room, filled with desks, chairs, and cabinets. The room was buzzing with activity, as SIS staff typed, filed, and sorted various documents and reports. She could hear the sound of telephones ringing, radios crackling, and voices whispering. She smelled the aroma of tea, coffee, tobacco, and ink.

She made her way to her own desk, which was near a window that overlooked the courtyard. She set down her coat and bag and poured herself a cup of coffee from a nearby pot. She looked around the room, trying to spot any familiar or friendly faces. She also looked for any signs of trouble or danger. She knew that working for the SIS was not without risks, especially now that she had something to hide. She felt a slight tingling in her talisman, and she knew that Eris was watching over her. She smiled and whispered to herself, "Good morning, auntie."

Eris made herself visible to Erin. She was sitting on the edge of her desk smiling at her. She gave her a little wink and whispered, "Good morning little sis."

"You are still my aunt."

Eris rolls her eyes, "Mortals. So hung up on labels"

Erin pulled the stack of papers that were in her tray and started scanning through them. Without looking up she tells her aunt quietly, "You know, those painters and sculptors didn't even try to do you justice." Erin peeks up at her, "You really are stunning."

Eris answers her excitedly, “I know! They make me look like something that crawled out of Hades. I may accidentally knock a statue over and break it from time to time.”

Eris leaned back and stretched out her long tan legs, letting her long red hair flow back touching Erin’s desk. Her back was arching and emphasizing her gifted shape.

She pops back up and leans towards Erin, still shuffling through papers.

“Find us something fun to do in there.”

Erin stopped and looked at her new aunt.

“I am beginning to form the opinion that you and I may have different definitions of the word fun?”

Erin pulls the papers from her coat pocket and lays them out on her desk, picking up the man’s photo ID. She reads the name, “Robert Smythe, well that couldn’t possibly be a cover name,” she remarks sarcastically.

“I know this face.” She looks at the image. She hadn’t really made the connection a few nights before in the dark bombed out building.

“I have seen him, but I can’t remember where”

“Seen who? And who are you talking to, Erin?”

She looks up to her coworker, who is now beside her. Eris is grinning, running her foot up and down beside his leg, not touching him but taunting Erin.

“I was just thinking out loud. Sorry. Say, do you recognize this man?”

He takes the ID from Erin’s hand and studies it, “Yes, I have seen him around. I think he works here. No, yes, he does work here.”

"REALLY? WHAT'S HIS name?" Erin asked, hoping to get more information from her coworker.

"His name is Peter Collins. He works in the cryptography department. He's a bit of a loner, but he seems to be good at his job. Why do you ask?" He replied, handing back the ID to Erin.

Erin looked at the ID again, comparing the name and the photo. She doubted that Peter Collins was his real name, he was just using another cover. Why were they following her? They didn't seem like they were up to anything good. She was pretty sure the gun the man had in his hand was clear evidence of that.

She decided to play it cool, and not reveal her suspicions. She smiled and said, "Oh, no reason. I just thought he looked familiar. Maybe I saw him in the cafeteria or something. Thanks for your help."

She glanced at Eris, who was still sitting on top of her desk, smirking. She could tell that Eris was enjoying the situation, and that she had something to say. She hoped that Eris would keep quiet, and not cause any trouble.

She turned her attention back to her coworker, who was a friendly and helpful man. His name was Henry Jones, and he worked in the analysis department. He was a tall and thin man, with brown hair and glasses. He wore a tweed suit and a bow tie, and he always carried a briefcase. He was a bit of a nerd, but he had a good sense of humor and a keen mind. He and Erin had worked together on several occasions, and they had developed a rapport.

He smiled and said, "You're welcome, Erin. Is there anything else I can do for you?"

Erin shook her head and said, "No, thank you, Henry. You've been very kind. I have to get back to work now. Have a nice day."

She watched him walk away, and then she looked at the papers on her desk. She looked around the room, desks and faces and the tops of heads, all clicking away at their jobs. And she could be certain now that some of them didn't belong here. Maybe not in this room, but someplace in this building.

She picked up the papers and put them back into her pocket. She stood up and grabbed her coat. She looked at Eris, and said, "Come on, auntie. Let's go have some fun."

Erin walked down the hall, holding some file folders that she didn't even take the time to look at. She just wanted something in her hands to make her look like she was doing something. Some prop to dissuade unwanted questions.

She stopped at a door with a black and gold metallic label on the glass, "Personnel". She stepped into the room and went straight to the counter, projecting confidence, as though she was exactly where she was supposed to be and doing exactly what she was supposed to do.

"Hi Judy. I need to get into the files and do some comparisons on a few of our men."

"Oh, sure, Erin, what is this pertaining to?"

"Come on, you know how this works. Compartmentalize. Need to know."

"Oh, it's that kind of thing. Ok, go on back. You know how to find what you need."

"Thanks Judy, one day we will sit down and have a long talk. Fill you in on the mysteries behind all the shadows and walls." Erin swings the small wooden gate to the side and goes past Judy into what was basically a library of cabinets.

She walked to the section starting with 'C' and began her search. 'Collins, Peter'. Recruited in July 1944. Spoke German and Russian. Decryption specialist.

She kept reading until she found another name. His recruiter. Another Agent, Roger Plank. Erin thought, "At least it wasn't Smith."

She closed the yellow folder and Eris whispered, "Erin." and took her hand. They were on the other side of the room, and she saw a man walking up to the cabinet she had just been in front of. It was still open, and he looked down, and started brushing through the tops of the folders.

Erin quickly shoved Peter Collins's folder into her bag and opened one of the others she had brought with her and sat down by a table.

He looked up and scanned around the room.

Erin held up the folder in her hand, covering her face from him, as though she were reading something.

The man closed the cabinet and walked away.

"He's gone." Eris tells her.

"That man was one of them." Erin says nervously.

"Well, let's get busy and find out who he is."

Erin went to the 'P' cabinets and pulled Roger Plank's folder. This was another face she saw that night. Now she was looking for other connections between the men. What missions did they share. And who was the third and fourth man. The man who was just in the room with her? And the one whose face she hadn't seen?

There were a few names that came up. Some of the same names that shared the same missions, and other names that turned out to be casualties on those missions.

The more she looked, the more she could see the pattern.

"How could no one notice this?" She asked Erin, as she filled her in on what she was seeing.

"Maybe someone doesn't want to notice it."

"We need to get out of here before anyone else comes looking. I am sure that man noticed the missing folder." Erin was worried now. She had no doubt the two of them could take care of themselves. But she had a family and friends. Her boys. The Carrigans. If she exposed herself, they would all be in danger.

She glances into Plank's folder one more time and her eye is caught by another name, Henry Foster. She recognized that one. But where?

"One more file, Eris. Then we go."

She rushed into the 'F' section and searched frantically, looking back over her shoulder at the counter and Judy, then back to the stiff paper sleeves. Foster, Henry. "There, let's go."

Erin shoved the folder into her bag, and Eris grabs her hand. The two vanish as footsteps stop at the closed door, opening on the face of Henry Foster and another man.

Erin and Eris appear in a bathroom, and Erin runs to the mirror. She is thinking, how do I make myself look different and not draw any attention?

She pulls her hair back and starts weaving braids, starting at the front and going back, like a soft crown of hair. Eris smiles and starts helping her.

"I could just take you out of the building." Eris offers her through the mirror.

"No, people need to see me leave. I can't risk any suspicion that I am onto anything."

She steps back and looks at her hair, and shrugs.

"Eris, you can take these out though," she pulled the folders from her bag and handed them to her aunt, "I can't risk being stopped and have those files found on me."

"Okay, I can do that. I will keep an eye on you and make sure you leave here with no problems too."

"Thanks. How is the fun working out so far?" Erin grins.

"Well, I think we have a good start."

Erin returned to her desk and pretended to work on some reports. She glanced at the clock and wondered how long she had to stay here before she could leave. The text in front of her was a blur, and the hands on the clock were at a crawl.

She heard footsteps behind her and turned to see a man in a dark suit and a hat. He had a stern face and a badge that identified him as Major Wilson, the head of the SIS. He dropped a thick folder on her desk and said, "Erin, I need you to clear these names for a meeting in Yalta. They are some of the top officials from the Allies. We need to make sure they are not compromised or under any threat. You have until tomorrow morning. Don't let me down."

He walked away without waiting for her reply. Erin opened the folder and saw a list of names, along with their photos and biographies. She recognized some of them as famous leaders and diplomats, such as Churchill, Roosevelt, Stalin, and Molotov. She thought, "Well these are obviously cleared," but she caught herself. Nothing was obvious now. Nothing was what it appeared. Her whole life was a play for the audience who couldn't see behind the curtain.

She also saw some names that she didn't know, but who seemed to be important figures in their respective countries.

She scanned the list and felt a jolt of shock when she saw one name: Henry Foster. He was listed as a liaison officer between the British and the American forces. His photo showed him smiling confidently, with a twinkle in his eyes. He looked nothing like the cold and ruthless spy that she had seen chasing her that night.

She felt a surge of anger and fear. How could he be involved in such a crucial meeting? What was his plan? Did he intend to sabotage the negotiations, or worse, kill someone? She had to do something. She had to stop him.

But how? She couldn't just accuse him without any proof. She couldn't risk exposing herself. She couldn't trust anyone in this place. She had to be careful and smart. She had to find out more.

She closed the folder and put it in her bag. The minute hand found its way, kicking and screaming in protest, directly to the twelve, on top of the hour hand. It was time to leave. She couldn't risk staying until the end of the day here. She was going to have to go back to Lyme Regis now.

She gathered her things and headed out of the office and down the corridor. Out in the streets she looked around and crossed the large intersection diagonally, reversing the course she had arrived on. Her bag was bundled under her arm, held tightly in the cold winter wind.

Her feet made small clicking sounds on the cold concrete walkway as she moved briskly away from number 2 Whitehall Court. The wind catching the bottom of her coat and dress, lifting them gently to pierce her skin.

"Where the hell is she?" Erin asked herself. She kept walking. Passing offices and small stores. She looked back over her shoulders, watching for anything unusual, anyone who seemed to linger behind her.

She stepped out past the end of one of the buildings in front of an alley and someone reached out and yanked her back into the empty roadway.

She struggled, holding tight to her folders. The man tried to get his hand on her mouth, and she bit down hard. He dropped a rag from his other hand and pulled his injured one away.

Eris reached out and took Erin's bag.

Erin looked at her, annoyed.

The man tried to approach again, and Erin's hand lit up and she put it on his chest. You could see his bones and veins for a moment, then he fell to the ground.

Erin squatted down to get a look at him, and Eris leaned over, mocking her, looking at the man too.

"You are a real piece of work, Eris."

Eris turned her head and looked at Erin with a big grin.

Erin went through the pockets and collected anything he had that might give her some insight into why he was here.

Eris decided to speak, but in her usual mischievous way, "So, more fun? Or do you want to take the fast train home?"

"Under the circumstances," She nodded to the body on the ground, "I think fast train."

The Chapman's home was a spacious and elegant estate, nestled in the hills outside of Lyme Regis. It had a long driveway, surrounded by manicured gardens and ancient trees. The house itself was a three-story brick building, with large windows and a slate roof. It had a classical and refined style, reflecting not so much Chapman's wealth and taste, as it did the importance of the people they knew and dealt with.

The large room they were in was on the first floor, at the back of the house. It was a combination of a living room and a study, with a fireplace, a bookcase, a sofa, and a desk. The most striking feature of the room was the rear wall, which was made up of glass doors and windows, exposing the view of the ocean. The room was filled with natural light and a fresh breeze mingled with a warm cherry scented pipe smoke, creating a contrast with the dark and cold winter outside. The room also had some personal touches, such as paintings, photographs, and souvenirs from the Chapman's travels and adventures.

Her father and Uncles and Grampy Craig were all sitting at the end of the room near the fireplace, puffing on their dark stained pipes and laughing and recounting their most recent adventure.

She quietly shook her head thinking, "They all knew. Everyone but me. I could kill them."

Erin spread out the folders on the table and pulled out Henry Foster's. She opened it and began studying, looking for clues.

"Erin, come on over here and listen to the excitement we had yesterday." Jasper called her from his leather chair.

"Dad, I can hear you all from here. I have to go through these files. It can't wait."

If you heard one of dad's seafaring adventures, you heard them all. He was the proud confident hero that rushed in to save the day, Uncle Blejack saves his hide. That should pretty much cover this one, except instead of some extinct ship of ancient history it will be the submarine this time.

And she wasn't far off. They disguised themselves as US Naval officers and boarded a submarine destroyer, then led them up into the cold waters of the Netherlands, making sure a supply convoy got to port with food and supplies. The number of Nazi ships they sent to the seafloor would always be a question, but not one she would get her mind trapped into finding an answer for.

The papers began to drift outwards from the folders into a long blanket of pages on the tabletop.

"Hi Erin."

Erin felt a rush of relief, hearing his voice, "Hi Grampy."

"You look like you have a lot on your mind, girl."

"You have no idea."

"Oh, you would be surprised how well I know the place you are in." He put his hand on her shoulder. "Mind if an old dog helps you out?"

"Of course not. I could use some fresh eyes. It is getting to be overwhelming. And I have dealt with so much heavier file loads than this one."

"Sounds to me like you are personally involved." he says it in a questioning tone. "Careful, Erin. That is when we make mistakes."

She stopped and looked at the old man. He was right. He had been in this game longer than anyone. And he had seen it go bad many times.

She shook her head, "You're right. Maybe you can help me find some answers. First, why are they after me? I am just an analyst, and aid. I have access, but they aren't trying to get my access. They are pretty intent on killing me, I think."

"It's that bad, is it?"

"Yes, Grampy, they have tried twice. And I am afraid for you and Grammy and my boys."

"Oh, you let Grampy Craig worry about that. Let's see what you have yourself into. What are these files?"

Erin starts pointing out the files of the men she has identified so far, and the folder with the names that she needs to clear for Yalta, which just happens to have one of the names on the list.

They sit and talk about it for a few minutes, Craig nodding his head, Erin airing out her thoughts.

"I think you have your answer right there, love." He points at the folders. "Not all of them, but the why is in your hands. Yalta."

Erin was suspecting that herself, and now she got a chill in her spine with Grampy seeing what she did.

"They know who you are, and that you are good at what you do. Look at what you did here. Not everyone would have put all of this together off one killer's identification with a fake name."

She stared at the old spy and waited.

"You are in their way. That's all. They want you out of the picture so they can slip an agent into your seat. Then they can clear Foster and whoever else they need to. You know what this means, right?"

"Yes, I am getting the big picture here." She nodded.

"They have plans for the meeting at Yalta. And you have to clear him, this Foster. You have to let him pass, and then find out who his contacts are. Stopping him won't stop whatever they are up to."

"Grampa, they are inside the SIS. I found three, I know there is a fourth. There has to be more."

"Hon, they are always inside the SIS. And we have ours inside their intel branches. It's all part of the game. We find them and eliminate them, or we use them. This time we will use Foster, but if you don't mind, I have some people on the outside that can handle this Plank fellow for us. We don't need him. And I want you to give me a list of everyone you don't know to be one hundred percent clean when you go through that Yalta checklist. I still have connections. And I don't want you to draw attention to yourself."

Erin hugs her favorite spymaster, "I love you Grampy. Thank you."

He smiled warmly and said, "You're welcome, Erin. What's family for? And I'm always here for you." He wiped a tear from her eye and said, "Now, let's get back to work. We have a lot to do. And not much time."

He went over the faces and names with her, drawing on his long history to help her spot things. They discussed Henry Foster, but he was not the only one. There were others, like the man in the alley, that she didn't have a line on yet. She had to clear Foster, and Craig would arrange it for her to be out of the office to follow him and hopefully unravel his plot and his connections. Something big was planned. And they needed to find out what before it was too late.

At the other end of the room, Jasper pulled a twelve-string guitar from a thick black case and began strumming. He stopped and twisted a knob, tuning a string here and there, then gave it another strum.

He began to put together a little bit of a shuffling rhythm. He looked at Paul, who had picked up another guitar. Paul nodded and joined him.

They played a blend of folk and blues, with a touch of Celtic flair. Their guitars sounded crisp and clear, weaving intricate melodies and harmonies. Blejack added some depth and rhythm with his bass, and Joey kept the tempo with his table-top percussion. It was a refreshing and original sound, unlike anything Erin had heard before.

Blejack grabbed a bass, that was leaning against the wall. He listened to Jasper and Paul and followed their rhythm. He added some depth and groove to their sound, with his low notes.

Joey tapped his fingers on the table in front of him. He wished he had a drum kit, but he had to improvise. He used a spoon and a fork, as drumsticks, and hit different objects on the table, as drums. He used a plate, as a snare, a cup, as a tom, and a pot, as a cymbal. He kept the tempo, with his makeshift percussion.

Jasper began to sing, and Paul and Joey joined in, adding some harmony.

What if you get to heaven
see all you love and know?
What if you stand before them
with all your lies exposed?

When will you find time
for the right time
to wash that bloody nose?

What if you see the judgment
of all the souls you hurt?
When they show you mercy...
Will you still feel the curse?

When will you find peace
for that broken piece

of shattered, withered soul?

What if you get your second chance
could you make things right again?
Would you learn the hard way
Escape was never in the plan...

Oh... you can't lie to love
Not to man or God above
You have only been lying to yourself.

Oh... you can't lie to love
Not to man or God above
You have only been lying to yourself.

THEY PLAYED THE SONG with passion and skill. They had been playing together for years. Something they added to the theater line-up along the way. They enjoyed the music, and forgot about their troubles, for a moment.

Erin watched them, with a smile on her face. She loved music, and she loved her family. She clapped her hands, and tapped her feet, along with the song. She felt a warm and happy feeling, in her chest.

They finished the song and looked at each other. They grinned and laughed. They all felt a sense of accomplishment, and satisfaction. They looked at Erin and saw her expression. She was beaming, and clapping.

"I love it, but I'm not sure the world is ready to hear it. I don't even know what style you would call that." She said with admiration.

Chapter 7: Tides of Black

Lyme Regis, England.
February 1, 1945

JOEY ARRIVED WITH THE truck, a Chevrolet with a large bed and sideboards, covered with canvas. Not a speed demon, but it was right for this job. It had a straight six and a four-speed transmission, dual rear wheels. A couple of favors had been punched into their cards to get this away from the military.

Everyone's luggage was loaded along with a few cameras and makeup cases.

Craig had pulled an all-niter with Erin, arranging covers and paperwork. This was going to be the riskiest mission any of them had undertaken. Straight through enemy territory. And with all of them, the potential for mistakes and problems was high.

Everything was happening so fast now. Since the day of the funeral, another critical mission had to happen within days or hours. The last 24 hours were all hands in the planning room. People leaving to take care of one or a dozen items, returning to be right back out the door.

Erin was getting a few minutes to rest her eyes before they all loaded into the back of the cargo truck and headed to Dover to catch the ferry. This was the first time they would all be together for a mission, and Erin was excited and worried at the same time. Her dad and uncles had no special abilities like herself. And her mother hadn't really revealed much. Only that she could shield them.

She knew she shouldn't underestimate Maeve, but she had only ever known her as a loving mother and a nurse and caretaker. And of course, she was a tremendous organizer. She had managed to raise herself while commanding a small army of doctors and nurses and putting together emergency clinics and shelters. But they were about to cross into Nazi territory. In plain view.

And where were the others? Eris said she was ready to go on her own, but this was an important mission. A few blips and they could all be in Crimea. Not riding on trains bumping into Gestapo or Nazi soldiers.

Maeve slid down onto the sofa next to her and leaned over onto Erin's shoulder. "I can read your worry all over your face, you know. You're going to have to hide that inside."

"Yes, I know mom. I am just letting myself have this moment before we go."

"What you are feeling now, your father and I lived with for decades. From the day we met we were finding the cracks around us to slide through and survive. And your uncles were right there with us. We all know how this works. We are going to make it there and we are going to do whatever we need to do."

"Mom?"

"Yes, Erin?"

"The Chapman's knew? At the funeral? And they let me stand there and die with a broken heart? And their tears were so real. They seemed so heartbroken too."

"They were heartbroken. For you and the boys. For not being able to tell you. You had to be real. Eyes were watching. And your pain made theirs real."

Maeve put her hand on her daughter's knee and gazed at her seriously.

"Hon, we couldn't exactly walk out of that building thirty years younger and just drive home. And there are other things at play too. We have to stay hidden. The old Jasper and Maeve are in that cemetery with the old Blejack."

Erin gave her mom the same look in return, "Mom, if anything were to happen to you there, I would lose total control. I don't think anyone would survive it."

"You just do your part and let me do mine. You find them, all of them. I will do what I always do. People love me, you know. Now let's go save the world."

Just then a Morgan cycle car pulled into the drive. The fabulous little all but a car was almost a throwback to a decade before. It looked like a roadster, but only had one wheel at the rear, beneath a boat tail style deck-lid. It was nearly a matching shade of burgundy to Blejack's Chrysler.

Three spoked wheels, the size you would see on a motorcycle carried it down the drive toward the men watching at the truck. The little v-twin two-cylinder engine hammering out its tune through a long pipe extending down the side at the bottom of the rocker panels. The bonnet was strapped down with leather straps on over the top and locked against a stainless tombstone style grill shell, which was behind the engine, sitting exposed to the elements in front.

John shut it off, and removed his goggles and cap, helping break the wind that found its way over the small, slanted windshield.

Jasper and the men went over to the car as he climbed out and started removing the straps. The mumbling and laughing ensued as he continued to raise the bonnet and pull out a small box.

John tilted his head, prodding them back to the tail of the truck where he opened it up to show them his new toys.

Inside were several small box-like things about the size and shape of a cigarette package. He held up some small things, not even as big as a marble, that had tiny wires hanging from them.

He started talking and pointing then plugged the wire into the small container, stuck one of the bulbs into an ear, and tucked the other into his shirt.

Erin and Maeve walked out, now curious about what he had brought them. And they listened to him continue his explanation.

"Once you have these in your ear and near your voice box, or mouth, you just press the speaker surround and twist. Press on it again and it will send a signal to the others. It will sound like static, but you will notice a slight pattern. If you hear the pattern, and it is safe, just push your own speaker and twist. You will have two-way communications."

He showed them which knob to press to key and send, and explained they had a short range, but were nearly undetectable by the Nazi radio signal sniffers.

John and Joey went over some makeup tips that could make the wires even more invisible to an onlooker and everyone reached into the box and got their setup.

"Blejack, come grab this other box. You know what's in here, so you can explain it on the way. You guys need to go now if you are going to make the ferry." Blejack shook his head and John led him back to the gaping mouth of his sporty little roadster.

John gave Maeve and Erin a hug as they all climbed into the back of the truck and Paul fired it off. He stood and watched the cargo rig clawing up the driveway and on into whatever lay ahead of them.

Everyone tried to find a comfortable place to rest in the back of the truck on the long and wearing four-hour drive to Dorset. Paul kept the truck between the ditches and Joey kept him company and awake. Some of them even got to sleep a few minutes at a time. The droning exhaust and whining of the large tires kept the will to have conversations well in check. With every shift of gears, the tone of the engine and transmission changed, bringing hope that the trip would be near its end.

It was a cold and dark night, as Paul drove the truck onto the ferry terminal in Dover. He could hear the wind howling and the waves crashing against the shore. He glanced at the clock on the dashboard. It was almost midnight, and this was the last ferry to Calais. He began to feel his nerves inside twitching as the adrenaline poured in, waking them up.

Military men were moving trucks onto the ferry, and walking around the bridge that attached the ferry to the dock. A sentry came toward the door and Paul dropped the window for him. They spoke a few words and Paul pointed him to the back of the truck where the other passengers were riding.

The man signaled him and Joey to follow him to the back of the truck and opened up the canvas that dropped over the rear.

"I need to see your identifications and passes." He requested firmly, wanting no nonsense tonight.

Everyone gathered their papers and moved to the tailgate, offering them to him.

He looked them over, pausing occasionally, asking questions. "All of you are press?"

"Yes," they all agreed.

Paul was getting a little antsy, expecting a nod and a waving hand when they got there. This sentry was actually doing his job.

"I am going to have to go call in on this, folks, just sit tight." he said, handing back their papers. "It'll just take a minute."

Paul got a chill. This wasn't supposed to happen. They needed to get out of the country without anyone noticing.

"Hey, Paul!" a voice came from behind him.

Paul looked back over his shoulder, a little startled. "Well, there you are. How have you been?"

"Just peachy, Paul." He looked at the other sentry, "They can go, they are pre-cleared."

The sentry saluted his superior and looked at him, puzzled, and he waved him over closer. "Not a word to anyone else, Operation Black Tide. Make sure they are on the ferry."

The man looked around at all of them and nodded his head, like he had an understanding now, and waved them forward as he walked back toward the ferry.

"What the hell is Black Tide?" Paul asked him.

"That is this truck and everyone inside it now. Someone pretty high up the chain got me out of bed tonight. I don't know what you are all up to, but good luck my old friend. Once you are over that water, you are on your own." he paused and reached into his pocket, "Well, almost on your own. I was told to give you this. When you get across and take the train to Paris, you call this number."

Paul took the small card and looked at the number.

"Paul, remember it and burn it, right here."

He glanced up from the paper and pulled out his lighter, clicked it off and set flames to the small white rectangle, holding it until it nearly hit his fingertip, then let it drop to the ground and ran his boot over it, smashing the ash into the rocky concrete drive.

"Done deal. See you when we get back Carl."

"You're going to see me sooner than that. I will be riding onto the Night Ferry with you."

Paul nodded and turned toward the cab. He watched Carl's feet lift off the ground as he climbed into the rear, then got into the truck and put them down the short drive onto the deck of the ferry.

The main deck of the ferry had 4 sets of tracks, each holding six sleeper cars or five luggage cars. These cars had started their trip in London, then they were broken down into sections and loaded onto the ferry using brake vans to help control them, and a locomotive that pushed them on. The whole affair took about a half an hour, getting them onto the rails, locking them down with chocks and chains and then removing the brake vans.

It would take about three hours to cross the channel, then another half an hour to unload at the quay on the other side. A large portable bridge would be linked to the ferry, called a linkspan. It had tracks attached to it that tied into the main line. Once connected to the locomotive, it was a direct run to Paris. It was all a pretty incredible feat of engineering. And the entire time, the cars were filled with sleeping passengers. Well, except economy class, now filled with soldiers, they would have to get out during the seafaring part of the trip and go to the upper deck.

Once the large ship had churned up its massive engines and pushed out into the dark water, everyone got out of the back and took a few minutes to stretch out and take in the night moon over the waters, now splashing against the bow of the large boat as it moved toward the shores of France.

He climbed out of the back and joined the others then whispered, "Okay, grab your things and follow me, in pairs. We will try to take advantage of the confusion as the soldiers make their way off the train and up onto the observation deck. You have become the benefactors of the Queen's blessing and first-class tickets." Carl passed out tickets and they set off across the deck.

They dodged around a section of army cargo trucks and jeeps, then walked beside the rail cars until they reached the blue cars with gold stripes and letters. He stopped next to one and motioned for them to start. Everyone crossed the short space between the trucks and the railcar two at a time, going up the steps into the door at the end of the car.

They each slipped into the first berth to the left, where the packages were being lifted inside. Joey lifted one of the bunks, closing it against the wall, making more room.

Inside and out of plain view, Carl went over a few small details that he had been given to pass on, then slid his way back to their truck to remove it at the end of the run.

Blejack spent the next hour passing out passports, currency, small tidbits like receipts and pawn tickets, photographs and other miscellaneous items. Thinks to make a person's backstory. They all knew how this worked. It wasn't likely they would need this complexity in their mission, but they would be prepared.

There were no loud pen guns for them. A single shot that required them to be right on top of their target. And a loud report that would give them away. They brought a little trick with them from the amazon. They had a pen, but it contained darts. Tiny little darts that were coated with the perspiration of their friend the dart frog. The pens functioned as a pen, but if they pressed it in the right place and twisted it the right way, the lever would release its venomous payload instead of its ball point quill.

It had its downsides. They called it the suicide pen. You could fire multiple darts in succession at close range. But once you fired it, even touching the pen where the darts exited could be fatal. Each one of them had a small cap they could place over the tip with clay inside that contained a neutralizing agent. A quick twist and they could not only clear the metallic outer edge, but also reseal the pen. But the best practice was to utilize it and destroy it.

Each of the pens had a case that had its lining coated in a reactive solution that would change color if somehow one of the pens were to leak. Then they would have only seconds to use their antidotes if they touched the poison by mistake.

"They couldn't spend the money for one more room?" Paul grumbled.

"There are two bunks, Paul." Jasper reassured him.

"Fine, Paul will share a room for you Cappy, anything for the Cappy, wash the feet for the Cappy?"

"One day, I am going to take you up on that foot wash, but until then, you know my response." Jasper gave him a smirk.

They had played this game for over forty years. He knew what Jasper had to say. "Piss off."

The men started to slowly filter out into the passage and go find their bunks. The berths had a decent sized bunk on each side as you stepped inside, with a light fixture and vent in the wall just above where your head would be, set into rich wood panels. The wall at the side of the bunk had a magazine pocket recessed into it, with a netted cover, holding in its stash of reading material. At this point, containing yesterday's news and a magazine.

The Night Ferry was a large icon of faith and hope between the British and the French. Creating a bridge between these two countries who had once been savage rivals. Now, in its gray paint and the black of night, every trip brought new reinforcements to the field to secure their neighbors' freedom, and each return carried the wounded.

It had been barely seven months since the ally's had landed on the coast of Normandy, and five months since the German garrison had surrendered in Paris. The fighting was still going strong. There were saboteurs and spies and SS troops who refused to acknowledge they were defeated.

People were already starting to act like it was over. Traveling and planning for tomorrow. If they didn't get to the conference and put a stop to whatever this plan was, it could change everything. If Churchill and Roosevelt didn't get an agreement from Stalin, he would press his advantage and overrun Europe while the other allies were looking at their calendars and setting dates and making plans.

For all of their anxiety and sense of urgency, there was no getting past the time it would take to travel. This wasn't new either. Maeve remembered the first time she battled the stillness before the world erupted around her. What they all referred to as the Battle of Shadows. Waiting in the Salamander out on the open sea for word on the pirate traitor, Ben Hornigold.

It seemed like they floated out there nearly in silence for a week. Afraid their voices might carry over the waters and alert their prey. And then it was cannons and sails and blood and screams. She made her place in that world on that day. Saving the lives of injured sailors.

She looked across the small chasm separating their two bunks at Jasper, still staring up at the ceiling. And then she got up and crossed it, pulling his blanket aside to crawl in with him.

"You know," she whispered, "there are a few other advantages to our sudden youthful transformation."

He turned his head to look into her eyes, "What do you think I was over here going over in my mind?"

They began kissing and she flipped off the small light over their heads. She remembered there were other things that had happened on that long quiet wait off the coast of New Spain that made it less tense.

ERIN WOKE EARLY, SHE had been fighting her own demons through the night. Sharing a mission with her family brought a new element of danger for her. She wouldn't be able to compartmentalize it if something were to go wrong and one of them were captured and tortured. She had powers she didn't really understand and couldn't reveal. And her new guardians hadn't been seen in nearly two days now.

They were on their own, it looked like. That part wasn't unfamiliar. She had been over the lines a few times. In countries she didn't know the languages of. Feeling like she was sticking out like a light inside a cave. The feeling could be overwhelming and if you didn't get it under control, you would definitely get yourself caught.

She got dressed and used the small lavatory to put on her make-up, brush her hair and try to hide the lack of sleep from her eyes.

She stepped into the passageway and could see the small light through the curtains of her parents' cabin, so she gave the door a light tap.

Jasper was in the tiny restroom shaving around his beard when he heard the soft knocking and popped his watch open to check the time. It was just after five am. Less than an hour until they would arrive in Paris.

Maeve peeked out at the edge of the curtain and opened the door. She motioned her inside, "Come in, we are up."

"Mom, I just wondered if you would like to have breakfast with me?" Erin asked her mom as she closed the door behind her.

"I would love that. Just give me a few minutes to get myself ready. Go ahead and order us some coffee if you want to. I will be right behind you."

Erin sits down near the door at the end of the dining car and orders coffee and toast. It only takes a few minutes for the kind man to return with her order.

She sits, happily sipping her coffee, taking in the officers and their aids sitting at the tables drinking their tea or coffee and eating breakfast. She notices a familiar shape at the other end of the car. He is sitting with another man she doesn't recognize. His back is to her, then as he bends down to pick up a small case, she recognizes his profile. It was Foster.

She ducks down into her bench seat and quickly turns on her tiny radio and sends a message to her mom, "Foster is here and I am trapped. He has someone with him, and I don't think I can get out without them seeing me."

Maeve answers her, "Can you hide? Cover yourself or anything? I will come and distract them."

Erin looks around and grabs one of the large cloth napkins and wraps it around her hair, she sees a newspaper on the table next to her. She grabs it and holds it up, covering her face with it, pretending to read it. She hopes that Foster and his accomplice won't notice her, or at least won't recognize her.

She hears the door of the dining car open and close. She peeks over the newspaper and sees Maeve enter the car. She looks different from before. She has changed her clothes and her hair, and she has put on some makeup and glasses. She looks like a sophisticated and elegant lady, who is traveling for business. She also looks very much like Erin, except for the small details.

Maeve holds her palm up to Erin, motioning her to stay put. Then she picks up the coffee that Erin had ordered for her and drops it onto the floor, making a loud fuss.

This immediately gets the attention of the two men, and she turns away and goes back out the door, not letting them get too close a look.

Erin carefully watches as Foster taps his associate on the hand and says something in German to him, and they get up and follow in the direction that Maeve had just gone, passing Erin, still holding the newspaper up over her face.

Erin quickly slips her foot into the closing door, then eases up and watches as the men pass through another door between the cars. She jumped up and followed them. She watched carefully from the edge of the small window and the men moved from cabin to cabin, looking inside for her.

Giving them time to move away from the door she had blocked, she opened it without being noticed. Then she slipped through and followed behind them.

Maeve waits for the two men between the next set of cars. Foster rushes toward her, thinking he had Erin cornered. As he the door closes behind him, Maeve uses something to block the latch so the second man can't get through.

Erin is not far behind and sees her mother is now trapped with this killer, and there is another man between them.

Foster grabs Maeve by the throat, shoving her against the wall of the train car, choking her. Maeve struggles, her hands desperately trying to force him away as she gasps for breath.

Erin runs at the second man, slamming her fist into the back of his head, not even thinking of her powers. He bends over and she shoves him with her foot. As he falls, she jumps over, trying to get to the door and her mom.

Maeve is punching at the man who is still trying to choke her. He is still unaware of Erin, who is trapped on the other side of the door.

The man on the floor pulls a gun with a silencer, and fires a shot, missing Erin and hitting the ceiling.

She turns back to him and kicks at the gun. The man rolls over and tries to get another shot off.

Erin dives onto him and they wrestle on the floor, barely wide enough for the two of them.

She gets an arm around his neck and starts to choke him, his eyes close as the oxygen is cut off from his brain.

Maeve is watching through the glass as she pushes back against Fosters hold on her own neck. Seeing Erin is about to lose their best hope of getting any information, she grabs Foster's pinky finger and bends it completely back against his hand, snapping the bone and cartilage.

Foster jerks back instinctively and blankets the broken finger with his other hand, losing his grip on her neck. Maeve kicks him full center in his chest, and he sails off the now slow-moving train into the field passing by.

She jerks the door open and yells to stop Erin.

"No, Erin, we need him!"

Erin lets go of him and shoves his limp body off of herself. She stands up and they both watch, wondering if it was too late.

Maeve says quietly, "Grab his feet, let's get him out of the hallway."

They started to drag the man down the hallway, and Maeve noticed a couple of young officers through the windows of the doors to the dining car, coming their way.

"Get Blejack, soldiers are coming." Maeve nodded her head to the right, indicating the door by Erin. Erin tapped rapidly on the door, hoping he would move fast to open it.

Blejack looked out the curtain, then snapped the door open and reached out to help Erin drag the limp body into his cabin.

He just got his head inside when the door at the end of the car opened up to the men chattering away.

Maeve gave the man's head an extra push then pulled the door shut. She smiled at the two men as she turned and went to her own cabin to get Jasper.

The four of them sat in the little room looking at the man on the floor.

"Well, this is a complication," Jasper noted as the two ladies recounted what had happened.

"We don't have enough time to work this guy over. I bet we are less than fifteen minutes from the station." Blejack assessed.

Jasper studied him and looked at Maeve and Erin.

"Okay, dope him, Blejack. It will be dark when we pull in. We will need to take him with us. Drop him down that hole, and we will slip out here and limp him away like he had too much to drink."

Jasper pointed to a section of the floor that had brass edging around it in a square about two feet square, and a small circle of brass, inset to allow a finger to pull on it. Some kind of maintenance access.

All three of them looked at Jasper like he had lost his mind.

Jasper looked back, "Maeve, you and Erin go with Paul and Joey. We will handle this alone. We will figure out where to put him and message you on the radios. Just don't get away too far from the station."

"And what if you are spotted?" Erin asked her dad.

"Well, he will become less valuable, and we will have to make tracks without him. Better it is just the two of us at risk. Relax, I have Blejack with me."

Maeve rubbed her neck, and Erin asked, "Are you okay, mom?"

"Yes, fine. I needed him to be watching me and not back inside the train to see you. I want him to think I am you for as long as possible. We can use that."

Jasper rubbed her shoulder and inspected her neck. "I hate to add more to your list, but you will need to take our bags to Paul and get them off the train with yours."

Blejack scribbled something on a tiny piece of paper and handed it to Maeve, "Call this number as soon as you get to a phone. Read this line to him and ask them to send us a covered truck or a sedan. Something with a good-sized boot."

They felt the brakes begin to engage, causing a light jerk.

Erin took her mom's arm. "Ready?"

"As ever." Maeve replied, missing her normal smile.

The two took Blejack's suitcase left the cabin and went down the hall to Paul and Joey's door.

They had dropped the man down under the train on the opposite side from the platform. Their car was near the rear of the train, but it might as well have been a hundred miles to the end and the nearest point they could get the man out of sight.

They had told Paul and Joey to try to tie up the policemen that were walking patrol long enough that they could find a way to get him out of the station. There wasn't much to work with. Several sets of tracks, another train that apparently was out of service. Dim lights only shadowed by the body of the rail cars gave them any kind of cover.

The only shot they had was a small service truck. Jasper legged it to it, keeping low and trying not to be spotted. He went around it and opened the driver's side door and looked quickly to see if there was a key in the ignition. First piece of luck, there was. A single key with a beaded chain attached to a small circle of paper with a metal rim. It simply had the number of the truck written on it in ink.

He started it up and pulled slowly alongside Blejack, who quickly opened the passenger door, stood there a moment looking at Jasper as though they were talking. Jasper watched the officers who were talking to Paul and Joey.

"Let's do it."

Blejack pulled the man up, and Jasper leaned across the seat, helping to drag his dead weight into the cab.

Blejack started to climb the step into the passenger seat.

"No, go with them. We won't risk any more than we have to."

"We don't have time for this, Jasper. You know that is horseshit." Blejack scowled.

"No, shut the door. Wait for my call."

Jasper put the truck into reverse.

Blejack looked at him hard.

"I can't back up with that door open cuz."

"You can be an asshole sometimes, Jasper."

"I can, but I won't bet my hand with your chips. If anything happens to me, they are going to need you. Go."

Blejack bit his annoyance down and shut the door quietly.

Jasper backed the truck slowly down alongside the rail cars to the end and turned it around, leaving around the end of the long platform.

Chapter 8: Peril in the Panthéon

Paris, France.
February 2, 1945

THEY SAT AT SOME TABLES at an outside cafe, just a block from the terminal. Paul and Blejack both discussing how they regretted leaving the truck on the ferry with Carl and not driving instead of taking the train. And they waited for their contact to arrive with something they hoped had room for all of them and their extra baggage.

Maeve and Erin sat at a separate table, with Joey at a third. The tables around them were filled with other morning coffee drinkers giving them a semblance of cover. Others who had gotten off the train were sitting with their own luggage, probably waiting on rides. Waiting out in the open didn't inspire a lot of confidence. They were working blindly and waiting on people they didn't know.

They could see around them a city that was trying to recover from the war, but still bore the scars and the signs of the occupation. Buildings that were damaged or destroyed by bombs, bullets, or fire. The streets were beginning to hum around them with people who were going to work or leaving a party. A city that was celebrating its liberation, but still faced the uncertainty and the hardship of living with their illusions stripped away.

Erin watched as a man across the street had unloaded some tools and mixed some kind of mortar in a handmade mixing box, two boards that had been cut at a curve on the ends, then sheet metal was nailed to the bottom forming a trough. He began using a trowel to scrape the mixture into holes and cracks in the front wall of a tailor's shop. She could barely make out the stained walk beneath where he worked, and the hairs stood up on her arms.

She looked around and asked herself the questions no one wanted to ask. How many of these people have had to hide for the last four years? How many desperately pleaded for a visa to escape what came? How many of these people pointed to their friends and neighbors when the police came looking? How many were happy to see them loaded into trucks and taken away? How many just watched as people were arrested for no reason except existing?

No, not all of this drink and noise was to celebrate the relief that the Nazi's were gone from Paris. Some of it was to try to drown the guilt, or the sorrow and loss. Europe was going to have to find a way to go forward from here. The papers were showing the extent of what the Nazi's had done in Poland now. They couldn't ignore the images on the front pages of the newspapers over the last few days.

Auschwitz had confirmed their worst fears. But it also seemed to motivate them. Even some who had witnessed or aided in the deportations. Now they were united to fight against the Nazi's and support the allies, not just to keep Paris free, not just France, but to free Europe. It would be a long road for Paris. A long road of mourning, justice and reconciliation.

But there was another question. In a world where so many chose to ignore, to justify, to betray for their own benefit, how long until they chose to forget?

Blejack and Paul got up and took several bags, Paul slightly more loaded than Blejack who kept one hand free. They headed down the street where they had been watching as man parked a covered truck and left them a mark on the tailgate. They made sure he had gotten into another car and left before approaching the rig.

They tossed their suitcases into the rear then got into the front and started the truck, sitting there. Joey finished his coffee then followed their steps, while Maeve and Erin lifted from their seats and went the opposite direction, turning the corner and walking toward the end of the block.

After Joey reached the truck and climbed inside, they went around the block and picked up the two women on the next street. This wasn't the best subterfuge they had pulled, but it was something. They didn't expect to have any eyes on them in Paris, but they wanted to make some effort to hide the fact they were all together.

Blejack was probably the most familiar with Paris, and it didn't take him long to find the place where Jasper had their bundle stashed. He pulled past the small alley and backed the truck into it, blocking the small utility truck's view from the street. They loaded the unconscious man into the bigger truck and pulled away, leaving the railroad's vehicle behind for someone else to find.

Joey asked Jasper, "How much longer will he be out?"

"I couldn't say for sure, but I imagine another hour at least. You never know with Blejack, maybe two days." He grinned recalling the last time Blejack gave him some help sleeping.

Blejack pulled down the streets nearing the airfield and brought the truck to a stop next to a brick building near the corner. He got out and walked around the truck, looking for eyes, then went back to the cab and flashed a short code on the headlights.

Ahead and across the road a large garage door began opening and he got into the cab and drove toward it and then inside. As the door closed behind and their eyes cleared, they could make out several men around the large building holding rifles.

Blejack got out and walked to a man who was approaching the front of the truck. They spoke a few words then the man held out his hand and introduced himself as Jack.

They pulled the flap on the back of the truck, and everyone got out except the sleeping lump they had picked up on the train.

Jack said they had something special for him upstairs. He had a few of his men pluck the man from the back and carry him up the steps and Jack led them behind.

The men took the spy and placed him into a bed in a room that appeared to be a hospital of sorts. They inserted a needle and tube into his arm with a saline solution drip. They looked around and noticed right away several men dressed in SS uniforms. Before they could say a word Jack reassured them that they were his men.

Jack began, "We don't have much time, so we are going to try to make him comfortable with his surroundings. We have a little medicine to help him relax and feel free to talk." Jack had a pretty good evil grin. He was a man who enjoyed his work, that was easy to see.

Erin and the others retreated into a room at the corner with windows and blinds. There was a speaker inside that let them hear what was going on at the bed and the blinds were nearly closed, but they could watch without being seen.

The "nurse" gave the man an agent to counteract the drug that Blejack had given him and then administered another into the saline solution. She was standing by him as his eyes opened, and she began to speak to him in German, reassuring him that he had been recovered and was in safe hands now.

She softened him up with her pleasant voice and smile then walked away to the next bed, appearing to assist another patient.

One of the men in an SS uniform came to his bed and pulled up a chair then began asking the man what had happened. The man was fooled, or the drug was working, or both. He described what had happened on the train, and then began to give names and descriptions of not just Foster, but two others who were on the train with him.

Jack carefully took down the details as the man unfolded his secrets like he was with old friends.

Henry Foster was a double agent who worked as a liaison officer between the British and the Americans. He has access to classified information, and he passes it to the Nazis. He is charming and charismatic, but also ruthless and cunning. He is the leader of the spy ring, and he reports directly to a high-ranking Nazi officer.

Alan Wright was the man whose face Erin didn't see that night. He was a radio operator who worked at the Admiralty. His job was to intercept and decode messages from the Allies and then he sends them to the Nazis. He was also responsible for planting false information and creating confusion among the allies. He was quiet and reserved, but also very skilled and loyal to his cause.

Dorothy Smith was a secretary who worked at the Foreign Office. She was a mole who infiltrated the diplomatic circles and gathered intelligence on the political and military affairs of the Allies. She was also involved in sabotage and assassination attempts. She was smart and attractive, but also cold and manipulative. She was also having an affair with Henry Foster.

As our interrogator began to go after descriptions, the man started coughing and our fake nazi went to get him a glass of water.

Erin and Jack quietly discussed the information, and she gave Jack a description of Foster and what little she saw of the man they knew now as Alan Wright.

As they were talking, they noticed the spy began to hack and was now starting to foam at the mouth.

Jack jumped up and burst out the door, looking around the room.

The crew rushed to the hospital room, where they saw the spy lying on the bed, his mouth foaming and his eyes wide open. He was convulsing violently, clutching his chest.

"What the hell?" Erin exclaimed, as she checked his pulse. "He's been poisoned!"

"Who did this?" Jack asked, looking around the room. "Where's Bernard? He was supposed to watch him?"

They spotted him heading toward the door on the opposite end of the room, trying to sneak out. He was pulling off his SS uniform and had a pistol in his hand.

"Hey, you!" Jack shouted, pointing his gun at him. "Stop right there!"

The underground man turned and fired a shot at Jack, who ducked behind a cabinet. The bullet missed him but shattered a window.

"Get him!" Erin yelled, as she and the others ran after him.

The betrayer ran down the corridor, pushing aside the faux nurses and patients who were in his way. He reached the stairs and descended quickly.

The crew followed him, dodging the obstacles and the people. They fired a few shots at him, but none of them hit him.

They reached the ground floor and saw the spy heading for the exit. He kicked open the door and ran outside, ramming a mop handle into the lever to slow them down.

The crew followed him, forcing the door open and saw him running down the street, toward a parked car. The man opened the car door and stepped inside.

"Damn, don't let him get away!" Jack aimed his gun at him. "Shoot him, before he drives off!"

They all fired at the car, hoping to hit the underground man, or the tires, or the engine. But they were too late. The car started and sped away.

"Shit, we lost him!" Tom cursed, as he lowered his gun.

"No, we didn't," Erin said, as she pointed to a motorcycle nearby. "Come on, let's go after him!"

She ran to the motorcycle and jumped on it. She started the engine and revved it a few times. "We can't let him get away. He has seen all of us. And he might have information on their mission."

Erin dropped it into gear and sped off after the car.

Jack pointed at another car and Jasper and Blejack jumped into it with him. They fired off down the road behind Erin, who was bent down and moving the bike as fast as she could change gears.

Erin drove the motorcycle at full speed, weaving through the traffic and the pedestrians. She kept her eyes on the car, which was getting farther and farther away.

"Damn it, he's too fast!" she muttered, as she honked the horn and swerved to avoid a truck. She was catching up, but it was taking too long.

Behind her in the car Jasper asked Jack, "Can you catch up to them?", as he held his foot to the floor. He had his gun ready, in case they got close enough to shoot.

"I'm trying, I'm trying!" Jack said, as he accelerated and changed lanes. "But he's got a head start, and she is faster than us both."

Erin saw the car take a right a block ahead of her and turned right at the corner she was at, hoping to run parallel and catch up and cut him off.

Jack, carrying Jasper and Blejack, caught up and passed behind her following the other man's path.

As Jack turned the corner, he could see down the street a large building with a dome and portico.

"There, he's heading for the Panthéon!" he said, as she pointed to the monument. "That's where we'll get him! The streets are blocked off for repairs."

Erin saw the man's car pull to a stop in front of the building as she was closing in from the side street. He had a small machine gun in his hand, and a backpack on his shoulder.

He ran inside as she dropped the bike and sailed after him.

Erin pulled a pistol from inside her dress and ran up the steps toward the entrance.

Jasper yelled, "Erin, wait! He is armed!"

She glanced at Jasper and shook her head, "I know!", she yelled back then slipped through the large doorway.

"I know, I know!" Erin said, as she reached the entrance of the Panthéon. She saw the underground man disappear inside the monument. She followed him, ignoring the warnings of the men behind her.

She entered the Panthéon and looked around. She saw a large circular hall, with a high ceiling and a dome. There were statues, paintings, and plaques, honoring the heroes and heroines of France. There was a replica of Foucault's pendulum, swinging from the center of the dome. She saw a staircase, leading to the crypt, where the remains of the distinguished French citizens were buried.

She also saw the man she had been chasing, hiding behind a pillar, aiming his machine gun at her.

"Erin, watch out!" Jack shouted, as he and Jasper entered the Panthéon. They took cover behind a statue and fired at the underground man.

The nazi spy fired back, spraying bullets at them. He hit the statue, the pillar, and the wall, but missed them.

Erin dove to the floor and slid behind another pillar on the same row the man was hiding.

He fired again, hitting the column that Jasper and Jack were behind.

"Ha, ha, ha!" he laughed, as he reloaded his gun. "You fools. You think you have stopped me? You think you can stop Foster? You think you can stop the Führer? You are nothing, nothing but insects, waiting to be crushed! We will succeed, for the glory of the Reich!"

He fired again, trying to hit them. And Erin slipped closer, hiding behind the next column.

Jack yelled out, "Cole, just give up. You can walk out of this alive. You know we can't let you leave here."

He fired again, hitting the pendulum, and making it swing faster.

The man laughed, "I am an agent of the Gestapo. I have been working for the Nazis, for Foster, for the Führer, for years. I have been infiltrating, manipulating, and betraying the underground, the resistance, and the allies. I have been feeding them false information, leading them into traps, and killing them. You think I will believe you won't kill me as soon as I step out into the open?"

Jack mocked the man, "So, you're not just a traitor, a coward, a murderer! But a full-fledged goose stepping nazi. I am still offering you the best shot you have."

Jack tried to ease his head out for a peek and the man ripped into the column with lead again.

The nazi laughed, and said, "You're wrong, you're wrong! I'm not a traitor, I'm not a coward, I'm not a murderer! I'm a hero, a patriot! I'm doing what I have to do, for the greater good, for the final victory! I'm doing what you can't do, what you won't do, what you don't understand!"

Erin was now opposite the spy on the same column.

Jack tried to keep the man distracted by talking, Jasper made a dash for the next column, trying to get him into a crossfire.

Lead chipped a path behind Jasper into the floor and walls and he tucked himself behind the column.

The spy laughed again, "You are already too late. In two days, Foster will change the course of the war. You think you have won? You think that the Reich will just fall before you? All we have to do is remove the fools who stand in the way and your people will all join us. You should be thanking us for doing what your people didn't have the courage to do."

Jasper leaned out firing at the man, and he tried to move around the column only to be met by Erin.

She put her palm on his chest and with a flash of her eyes, a bolt of electricity ran through his body, and he fell to the floor. She focused on his chest and his heart collapsed inside his rib cage.

Jasper ran to her side, and Jack stood out in the open, noticing the bright blue light against the wall and ceiling.

"What the hell was that?" he asked.

Erin looked at him and shrugged, "Sorry, Jack. Classified."

Blejack stepped into the large room and gave them a sharp whistle. "We need to go. People are gathering out front and the police are on the way."

Jasper grabbed the pack the man had been carrying and they quickly went through his pockets and followed Blejack to the rear of the building.

They stepped out and walked toward the small group that had gathered near the entrance, acting the part of curious onlookers.

As the people pointed and talked, they eased themselves back down the side street that Erin had arrived on and kept walking, back to the warehouse.

As they moved away from where the action had taken place, Jack finally mentioned, "We might have gotten some information from him."

Erin shook her head, "He isn't the type that talks. And he was right, we are out of time."

She looked at Blejack, "We are going to need a faster ride, uncle Bleej."

"Already started making the calls, Button. The rails from here to there are a mess."

"We have less than 24 hours now. How soon can we get a plane?"

He shook his head slowly, "Well, it's tough to say yet. He had a worried expression on his face, and a frustrated tone in his voice. "I've been trying, but it's not easy. The air traffic is busy, and the security is tight. The military is busy, and civilians with planes are scarce. The planes are rare, and the pilots are expensive."

When they got back to the safe-house, Blejack sat down with the phone and a map. He dialed several numbers, coming up with no answer.

"Blejack, we need that plane," Erin said, as she looked at the map. He had been trying all of his regular contacts, to arrange their transport.

"I know, I know," Blejack said, as he nodded.

He looked at the map and pointed to their location. They were in Paris, France, about 3,000 kilometers (about twice the distance from Florida to New York City) away from Yalta, Crimea.

He held the receiver in his hand and paused before dialing another number, almost with a sense of dread on his face.

A woman's voice answered and Blejack turned on his happy voice.

"Matty? How have you been?" he began.

And she shut him down, "Blejack! You have a lot of nerve calling me."

"I know, I can explain when we meet, but I need your help."

"Who says I am meeting you?" She fired back at him.

"I promise, you will understand when I tell you. But we need your help and your airplane. It's a cash job and it is immediate." He put on all the butter and syrup as he tried to calm Matty on the other end of the phone.

"I don't think I want to work for you, Blejack. You always bring trouble."

"Matty, it isn't for me. It's for Maeve and Jasper."

She got quiet a minute, then answered, "If it is for Maeve, you know where to meet me. She had better be with you though."

"She will be. You had better prep with an extra tank and make sure they are all topped off."

"Blejack, you had better not be trying to take me into a hornets nest this time." She growled.

"No, it should be a clean run. We will show you when we get there."

"Ok, tomorrow morning at 7 a.m. you be standing where you usually stand." She hung the phone up before he could say another word.

Jasper leaned back in his chair with a big grin on his face, "I told you to call her."

"Every time I call her, she nearly gets me killed." Blejack shook his head. "I hope I didn't just sign us all up for a crash and burn."

"She is going to be surprised to see you this time. Better try to look older." Jasper continued to grin.

"Oh hell, that is going to be a problem." Blejack's face went serious, remembering the transformation he had gone through since he last saw the feisty little blonde pilot. "Well, at least we are closer in age now."

Jasper leaned his head forward, clasping his hands around the back of his head, "This is going to be fun."

Erin and Maeve both shook their heads. "Oh yes, loads of it." Maeve added.

They had all worked with Matty for several years since the war started. She was trustworthy, but a mess. Nothing ever went to plan with her. And now, she was about to be in for a shock, seeing her old friends had their clocks turned back thirty years. That would probably turn her chaos dial up a few notches.

Chapter 9: Blejack's Folly

Paris, France.
February 3, 1945

THEY SAT IN THE TRUCK and Jasper asked Blejack, "Well, how are we going to explain this to her, cuz?"

"I say we dart her and take her plane. It sure would be a lot simpler." Blejack grinned.

"No, you are not darting Matty!" Maeve jumped in. "I will talk to her. You two knuckleheads just stay out of the way."

Jasper held his hands up in surrender, "I didn't say we were going to dart her. Just listening for suggestions."

Maeve looked at Blejack, "Get out there and make the meet, and do not dart her."

"It wouldn't hurt her. Just keep her quiet for a while." He climbed out the back of the truck, "You might wish you had let me in a few minutes." He grinned at Maeve and pulled his hat down over his forehead and walked around the corner.

He went a few yards then stepped off the walk and back under a tree and waited.

A few minutes went past, and a green sedan came down the road. A nice-looking woman with blonde hair, wearing a flight jacket and cap was driving. She gave the headlights one quick flash and went on past. He watched her pull to the side of the street about a block away, then went back to the truck.

He slapped his hand on the hood and hopped into the passenger side of the cab.

"Pull around and follow that car that is parked on the side." he told Paul.

Paul slid it into gear and did as Blejack had instructed.

They slowed as they got near the car, and she pulled out and led them down the street to a gate.

She spoke to the sentry for a few minutes then waved for them to follow her inside.

She parked and got out and started walking, heading for the Douglas C-47 sitting with the stairs at the door. She was ready to go. Matty didn't fool around. Whatever planning you needed to talk to her about, you did that in the air.

Matty wasn't tall. She was maybe 5'6" after a good sleep. She had wavy blonde hair tucked up into her flight cap. There was a tan cotton shirt that buttoned up from her mid chest, not quite buttoned up, beneath her leather flight jacket. A pair of khaki trousers held at her waist with a tightly woven cloth belt.

Blejack and the rest climbed out of the truck and headed after her.

She stood at the bottom of the steps with her mouth hanging slightly open, not saying a word. But her face said clearly, she was bewildered.

Erin walked onto the steps last, catching Matty's blue eyes that seemed to be screaming, "What the hell?". Erin was the only one that made sense. Erin tilted her head, telling Matty to come onboard.

She climbed up and turned, pulling the door shut. Then she looked at them all sitting there, acting like nothing was wrong.

"Ok, someone had damn well better tell me what the hell is going on here, right now!"

Both Maeve and Erin closed up on her sides, taking her by the arm and leading her to the cockpit.

"We can't talk with these clowns," Maeve told her, "Men don't know how to communicate."

Blejack called from behind, "We could already be taxiing down the runway, Maeve." He had a real 'cat that ate the canary' grin on his face this time.

Maeve turned and glared at him.

"I'm just sayin'."

They were in the cockpit for a good ten minutes before they started to emerge again. They muttered a few things and Maeve walked back to sit with Jasper, Erin stood there, behind Matty, who was now flagging Blejack with her index finger to come to her.

He smiled and started walking to her, thinking everything was fine now, Maeve had worked it all out.

Then Matty swung her full body behind her little fist right into his jaw.

Blejack took two steps back and put his hand on his chin. "Damn, Matty, what did you do that for?"

"Dart me? You asshole!"

"Hey, they knew I was kidding. I would never dart you."

"You damned ass, you already did dart me before."

"Well, that was an accident. And it did keep you from being shot." He was still rubbing his chin.

"You should have called me. I could have been with you. How could you leave me out of being bombed with you?" If eyes were knives, she was slicing him up like thin ham. "Just don't talk to me." She turned back to the cockpit and started walking.

"You look nice." Blejack told her, hoping to soften her up or light her fuse.

She paused a second, then growled and pulled the curtain behind her.

Blejack sat down across from Jasper, next to Paul, "I am for sure going to dart her."

Jasper laughed and Maeve slapped his hands for laughing. Then Paul and Joey joined him.

The engines began to wind up one after the other, and the small cargo plane began pulling out onto the runway.

Erin came back to the back and strapped in.

"How long?" Jasper asked.

"Probably about 12 hours. She needs to make a stop in Bucharest to unload and refuel."

"So, we are looking at about seven hours to the fuel stop." Jasper nodded, feeling better about their mission now.

Erin smiled, "Not counting Matty incidents."

Blejack held up a small black case that he kept his tranquilizer darts in so Jasper could see it.

Jasper started to laugh again.

Erin looked behind her to see what her uncle was doing that was so funny, and he had his small case put away and acted as though he had suddenly fallen asleep.

"You are both children." She said, speaking in Blejack's direction.

Blejack kept his eyes closed and smiled.

The engines wound up and they started the rush toward take off. The vibration from the tires reverberated through the plane. Then the nose tipped upwards, and the heavy hydraulics pulled the wheels up and closed the doors over them.

Matty continued to climb for a good five minutes then she levelled the plane and began her turn to the east.

As the plane flew over the darkened and war-torn landscape of Europe, the passengers tried to relax and get some rest. Jasper and Maeve cuddled up in their seats, holding hands and whispering softly. Erin took out a book from her backpack and started to read, occasionally glancing at the window. Paul and Joey played cards, betting with chocolate bars and cigarettes. Blejack pretended to sleep, but he was actually listening to the radio chatter from the cockpit, trying to figure out what Matty was up to.

Matty was busy flying the plane, but she was also thinking about the strange and shocking situation she was in. She couldn't believe that Blejack and his friends were the same people she had met three years ago, when they were running from the Nazis in France. They looked so much younger, as if they hadn't aged a day in thirty years. And they had told her some unbelievable stories about time travel, Greek gods, and magic powers. She didn't know what to make of it all. She was angry, confused, and curious at the same time.

Blejack stepped into the cockpit past the curtain that was hanging in the doorway. He took the copilot's seat and said, "When are you going to get a copilot, Matty?"

"I am not. I now have trust issues."

"Matty, how was that going to work out? You and a sixty-five-year-old man, worn down from the sea and on the edge of being shot every day?"

She glanced over at him, "A year? You didn't contact me for a year. I told you how I felt, and you just disappeared on me."

"That's not all on me, and you know it. You know how this job works."

Matty turned toward him with a sad look in her eyes. "Well, why would you want me now? You are young and strong and can get any woman you want."

Blejack's mouth dropped open and there was a smile at the corners of his lips, "Are you kidding me?"

He got up and leaned over her, planting his lips on hers. She held the yoke with one hand as she let her head fall back and put her arm around him.

A few tears fell from her eyes as she inadvertently let the plane drift off course. She pushed him away, gasping for a breath, "Stop, I have to fly this thing."

She turned her attention back to the nose of the plane and the gauges when she noticed another plane on her right, just to the rear of her wings, a few hundred yards away.

"What in the hell have you guys gotten me into?"

Blejack leaned over to look out her window and saw the other plane, a German Junkers Ju 52, a three-engine transport aircraft that was used by the Luftwaffe. It had a red cross on its wings and a swastika on its tail. It was flying above and behind them, keeping a safe distance.

It had been trailing them for who knows how long. If not for their kiss causing Matty to veer off her course, they might never have noticed it.

They saw the side door of the plane open, and a man standing in it. He had a rope around his waist, and a long knife in his hand. Blejack recognized him from a picture in the field of papers that Erin had spread out on the table a few days before.

The plane started gaining elevation on theirs and the man looked down at them with a smirk and waved his knife. He jumped out of the plane and swung down towards the C-47.

The man swung in the air, hanging above them and Matty increased the speed. He slowly drifted back out of view of their windows, now over the body of the aircraft.

Matty began to tilt the plane to the left, away from the other plane and the man landed on the roof and stabbed his knife into the metal.

Blejack looked at Matty, "See if you can lose that bird, I will go see if I can get rid of our guest."

He held onto whatever he could, trying to walk as Matty steered the plane at angles trying to break the trail of the other plane, and maybe dislodge the man stuck to the outside.

"Jasper, we have company. One of Erin's friends." He pointed to the long blade protruding down through the shell of the roof.

Erin unbuckled herself, "I got this." She said as she stepped up and her eyes started to glow.

"No, no... Erin, you will short out everything on the plane." Blejack warned.

The man up top started sliding the blade in and out of the roof, trying to make a larger hole.

"Ok, that isn't going to work for us." Jasper said.

Blejack went to the wall near the cockpit and tried to climb his way up to an access panel in the roof while Jasper looked for something to work with.

Paul and Joey were just getting their minds around what was happening stuffing their cards into their pockets.

Maeve reached out a pair of large channel lock pliers to Jasper.

Jasper took them and smiled, giving her a nod.

Matty was still wrestling the plane up front, swinging the floor beneath them in the back. The other plane was glued to her tail.

Jasper and Paul were both trying to reach the knife in the ceiling from either end of the plane, both falling and sometimes floating their way towards it.

Matty put the nose up and Jasper grabbed onto a seat, his legs dangling now toward the rear of the plane. Paul slid back to the rear, catching Joey on the way. Blejack was hanging from the edge of the access panel opening, now with its small door hanging open.

Jasper yelled toward Blejack, “Is she trying to stall it?”

He was hanging with both hands and his left hand still held the pliers.

Erin studied on the scene then she stepped into the middle of the walkway and slid down toward the back of the plane.

She reached out and snatched the pliers as she passed her dad, then jumped toward the ceiling.

She caught the knife and dropped her weight on it, pulling it through the roof.

The man above was hanging by one hand clasped inside the edge of the hole he had made, and now his other fingers came inside.

Erin had landed on a crate that was strapped to the floor and made several jumps onto others, bringing her closer to the now bleeding palms.

She turned the knife and rammed it straight up through the metal, piercing the hand that wasn’t bleeding yet. When she pulled it back, he had let go, and she slammed it through his other hand.

This time when she drew the blade back, it was followed by the loud thumping of his body falling against the metal hull. He bounced his way down and against the tail fin, through the air and right into the prop of the other plane's left engine.

The plane that was trying to keep up with Matty suddenly went into a roll to one side and left a trail of smoke as the pilot struggled to bring his keel level again.

“Matty, level out and go!” Erin yelled.

Blejack repeated the message for Erin, trying to overcome the loud roar of her engines and the wind now coming through the hole in the roof.

She still climbed and Maeve, the only one not swinging from something in the cargo hold, began to crawl her way to the cockpit.

"Matty, we are clear, find someplace to land before we rip wide open!"

Matty leveled the plane and began her descent, looking for a landmark that could tell her where they were or a field to land in.

Paul watched the hole in the ceiling where the man had done the damage and could see it was still tearing now.

He looked around for something he could use to stop it or patch it, anything.

"Erin, I need the pliers!" he yelled against the howling noise.

Erin turned and looked at him, and his pointing finger. She saw the hole and ran to him with the pliers.

"The knife too?" he asked.

She looked around to see where she had thrown it and went to get it for him.

Paul began to try to take a sheet of metal off the bulkhead, removing bolts and screws and pounding away at small rivets. Joey joined in with him, pulling on the small panel as Paul beat away the little dots of aluminum.

Paul laid the sheet on the floor and began to use the tip of the blade to make small holes, spinning the blade so they would be round and not want to tear when he put screws to it.

"See if Matty has a flathead screwdriver, Joey, and hurry."

"Right away." Joey went at a run for the cockpit, passing the hole that was slowly growing above them.

Paul used his leg to round the metal slightly, and test fit it against the ceiling. Joey came hurrying back with a screwdriver.

"Hope this works, it's the only one she had." Joey held it out to Paul.

Paul held the sheet to the ceiling with one hand, taking the tool, "Hold this up for me. Keep it tight where I put the screws through."

They worked away at the patch, Joey keeping pressure wherever Paul pointed. He quickly worked his way around the metal scab until they couldn't find any more screws.

They looked at the fix, now blocking most of the wind noise, but still flexing and making the occasional popping noise and the metal was stressed.

"She better get us on the ground pretty soon, we are going to need a new plane." Paul wiped the cold sweat from his brow with his hand and rubbed it on his sleeve.

He walked to the front of the plane and stuck his head inside the cockpit to bring Matty up to speed on the repair. Blejack and Erin were both there, looking through her papers, identifying the man that favored himself an acrobat.

They found him. It was among the pages her grandfather had given her of Foster's associates. Alan Wright. The man who had managed to hide his face from her view when all of this had started.

They were half celebrating that they might only be down to two now, Henry Foster and the woman, Dorothy Smith. But they had no idea what she looked like. Only that she was attractive, and she was involved with Foster.

Matty pointed down at a field and there was what was left of a U. S. Army bomber scattered at the edge.

"This is as good as we are going to get, Blejack, do you think you and the boys can rob what we need from that wreck?"

Blejack looked at Paul, "What do you think, you seem to be our aircraft mechanic now?"

He shrugged, "We gotta' do something, might as well do that."

"Better strap in and hope I don't break us in half landing down there." Matty pointed her thumb toward the back of the plane.

While Matty circled around to make a stab at landing on the field below, Blejack helped Erin gather her papers and get them back into her pouch. Erin and Paul both went to the seats in the rear and strapped themselves in. Blejack took the copilots seat again.

"You might have to help me here. Just do what I say and when I say it, okay?"

Blejack gave her a nod, and she said, "Let's do this then."

She turned the nose down and started to bring the plane lower, "When I tell you, pull back on the yoke. We have to keep our nose up. But not too soon. Wait for me to say when."

"Ok, I got it. Bring us in Blondie."

Matty leveled out a few feet from the ground, then pulled back the throttle, increasing the engine speed, "Now, keep it straight and pull."

The tires barked against the grass and dirt below, causing the nose to try to dive forward as they caught on a section of ground that was hard enough to provide traction.

"Keep it tight, Blejack," she said calmly.

"Oh, I got this, you just keep us out of that line of trees."

Matty started dropping the throttle and the tail wheel hit the ground. She dumped the power, bringing the engines back down to an idle.

She turned the nose of the plane back toward the open field and the injured aircraft bounced and rolled to a stop.

Matty lowered the rear cargo doors then she shut down the engines one at a time and the quiet began to close in around them.

"Everyone still alive back there?" she called to them, turning her head toward the doorway.

"Seems like it, although I was never that sure about Paul before." Jasper answered.

Chapter 10: Matty's Affliction

Someplace on the Swiss Plateau, Switzerland.
February 3, 1945

JASPER, PAUL AND JOEY started walking across the field toward the wreck of the B17 to harvest some of its skin while the others began to gather tools from the rear of the plane.

Matty is pretty well equipped. Flying in and out of enemy lines has prepared her for making emergency landings and repairs on the fly.

She had a medium sized toolbox with hammers, chisels, punches, metal snips, and several large boxes of rivets.

She pointed Blejack to a ladder while she collected all of the tools that she thought they would need.

He set it on the wing, and she shook her head, "Not on there, take it around the front so we don't damage the flaps. We will never get back off the ground."

"You're the boss, Blondie." He smiled and moved the ladder around to the front of the wing.

Matty climbed up the ladder onto the wing and looked at the tear in the fuselage, and the dents the man left going back to and on the tail fin.

"The things I do for you guys." she shook her head.

It was bad, but manageable. She crawled up onto the top as Blejack joined her on the wing. "Keep your weight spread out, legs wide," she instructed.

"Aye, how bad is it?"

"It's bad. We're lucky we found this field."

She stepped wide across the tear and walked toward the rear, inspecting the other damage.

Blejack climbed up onto the roof, being careful to keep his legs apart. He walked gingerly toward the crack, and Matty.

He put a foot down out past the end of the tear, and just as Matty was about to stop him, he put his weight down. The metal ripped and his leg dropped through the new extension.

Matty didn't say a word, just slapped her palm onto her forehead and looked down, avoiding seeing Blejack stuck into her plane, one leg in, one leg out.

She walked up to him and held her hand out, "That is what we call 'metal fatigue'. Anytime you lose structure, the metal around it will have to work twice as hard. It wouldn't have taken long for the plane to break in half if we had stayed in the air."

"I think I get the picture," he smiled and tried to pull his leg free. "Yeah, this is a no go. Going to need some help from below to get my leg free of the metal."

"Ok, sit tight and I will go down and get some help for us."

She went down and had a few words with Maeve and Erin, who could already see the problem from inside.

"I will stand on this crate and hold the metal out, if one of you could go up and help pull him loose."

Erin answers her, "I can manage that for you. Or we could just put the new metal over him."

"Well, that is a good thought, but it might cut into my fuel consumption. We better get him loose."

Erin went up the ladder and climbed up. She stepped across the gash and turned to reach for Blejack's hand.

"You ready?" she asked?

"Any time you are."

"No, I meant Matty."

"Yes," she answered from below, "go ahead."

Erin gave Blejack a pull as Matty held the sharp metal away from his leg. And then she let him back down.

She held her finger to her lips, telling Blejack to not say anything. Then her eyes started to glow. The blue flame drew rune trails on her skin and her wings burst out in a blue blaze.

She grabbed Blejack by both hands this time and lifted him through the hole, setting him back down on the wing.

Inside, Matty saw her friend as Blejack opened up the skylight.

She muttered, "I really need a drink."

Erin landed on the ground and hid away her feathery sails, and Matty came walking out of the cargo bay.

"You got any more surprises I might want to know about?"

Matty wanted Erin to know she had seen her in action. And she also wanted to know what else she hadn't been told.

"Really, that is one of the best ones. You probably don't want to see the others."

She held out one of her hands and showed Matty. Her palm started to glow then electricity crackled around it, forming a ball of light. She turned and spotted a piece of the B17 wreckage farther away from the men and threw the globe toward it.

The ball of light hit the piece of wreckage and expanded across it, burning a large hole through the entire width of the section of broken aircraft.

"Does it hurt?" was all that Matty could think of saying.

"Not me." Erin grinned, "It does a number on the receiving end. It does give me a weird tingling through my body, but I am starting to get used to it."

"If I didn't know you so well, I would be terrified."

"Yeah, me too." Erin replied.

"Someday, you are going to have to tell me the whole story, Erin."

"Believe it or not, I have a book on it." she smiled, thinking of the book that Joey had given her boys at the funeral. "We get through with this trip, I will let you read it."

Blejack had finished setting the tools and rivets up onto the wing and Matty caught him walking back and put her arms around him and held him there.

Jasper and Paul and Joey were just coming back, carrying their replacement metal.

"Blejack, why don't you two go for a walk or take a nap or something. We will get this patched up here shortly." Jasper goaded him, nudging them out of the way of the ladder.

"Sounds like a good idea." He took Matty's hand and led her away from the plane while the others began climbing and lifting the panel up onto the wing.

Erin watched the unlikely couple walking away, Matty's head bobbing against his arm as she held it with both hands. She thought to herself, maybe when this was all over, those two might actually have a chance. They both deserve it.

The rest of them pounded out rivets and drilled holes in the new panel. One set the rivets in the top and another held a brace from below while the first hammered against it, sealing up the metal.

It was a good hour before they all came back down, and the plane looked like it was ready for service again. All the tools were put back and ready to go when Matty and Blejack made their appearance.

Erin had lost track of them sometime during the repairs. But she did notice them coming back from the tree line.

"They must have gone for the nap option," she thought and grinned.

Matty fired off the engines one at a time, watching the gauges, she set the engines at high idle and then engaged the rear door lift.

"This is going to be a rough one." She told Blejack, who had made himself copilot by now.

"You know I don't mind a rough ride."

Matty didn't look at him, but she smiled and shoved the throttle open.

She hadn't exaggerated. The rutted field nearly shook Erin's teeth loose. But they finally caught air under the wings and were back on their way.

She looked back at the new section of ceiling, and it seemed like it was as good as it ever was. Paul and Joey already had their cards back out. Jasper and Maeve were resting their heads together.

"Time for some rest now," she thought, and she closed her eyes and leaned back against an olive-green duffle bag that she was pretty sure contained Matty's dirty laundry by the smell.

"Oh well, bad sleep is better than no sleep." And she nodded off.

Yalta, Crimea.
February 4, 1945

WHEN SHE WOKE UP, SHE could hear Matty talking to the tower at the airfield. She was explaining that she was only carrying passenger cargo with a press envoy. They had been circling for several minutes already, and she finally got landing clearance.

Erin looked around and saw that Paul and Joey were asleep at the rear, and Jasper and Maeve were just waking up.

She tried to piece together how long she had slept. But after several minutes, she saw the task was too daunting for her right now. It seemed like days since she had slept. An hour here, two hours there. One battle after the next. But she felt rested now, even with her spine broken in a dozen places. Ten of those in the neck region.

Matty called back from the cockpit, "I am taking her in, so hold onto whatever is left back there."

Erin noticed there wasn't much. Matty had managed to land, unload her cargo, refuel and take off again and not wake her.

She sat up and gave her belt a tug, making sure it was still clamped around her. She leaned back, resting her head against the cold sheet metal wall.

"Today was it," she thought, "Today they either stop these spies or the war goes on for who knows how long."

She let her mind wake up slowly, trying to keep the anxiety at bay for as long as possible. She kept telling herself, "This nothing new. This is the job. We get in and do it and get out. Just like always."

The fat rubber tires barked on the pavement, shaking Erin in her seat. Her head rolled slightly forward and then back. Then they did it again, several times before the plane leveled out on the ground and Matty brought the plane to a gentle roll.

She taxied off the runway and brought the engines down, finally shutting them off.

Matty had stayed at the yoke all night. Blejack had kept her company up front, and awake. It was nearly morning now, the sky was showing a hint of blue, and the temperature was chilling.

She came to the rear and opened the door on the side of the plane, waiting for the crew on the ground to bring them a ladder cart.

Erin released her bindings and went to stand with her, "You alright, Matty? You must be exhausted."

"Oh yeah, both." She smiled, her eyes showing the miles.

"Get some sleep while we are gone. I have the feeling we are going to need a quick take off when we get back."

"Yeah, like you are saying something new. Remember that time we sat at the airfield and had wine and cheese before we took to the sky?"

Erin studied her, "No, not something I recall."

"Right, because that never happened. It's always dodging bullets with you and never enough runway and bad weather and someone tearing holes in my plane."

She gave Erin a hard look then broke into a smile.

Erin smiled back. "Well, you have expectations."

IT WAS STILL DARK WHEN Matty landed her c-47 and taxied off the runway. She had been flying for nearly 20 hours since Paris, not counting the emergency landing to patch the roof where the nazi spy had tried to carve his way inside at 9,000 feet, and the stop at Bucharest to refuel and unload cargo.

Erin made a phone call, using a number that she was given by Craig back in Lyme Regis and arranged a car for them. Everyone else got their gadgets together and disguises on.

Her anxiety had begun to build now. They had been in a dead rush to get here in time, and now that they were here, all she could think of was everything that could possibly go wrong. And not having a real plan locked in, that meant everything could go wrong.

As the rest of the gang leave for the conference, disguised as members of the press, Matty finds a spot on the plane and tries to get some sleep.

Erin takes in the atmosphere and scenery as the six of them sit crowded into the staff car. The sentry gives Jasper directions then waves them through to the street.

Erin looked out of the window as the car sped along the narrow road. The dark silhouettes of the Crimean Mountains loomed over the horizon, and the faint glimmer of the Black Sea was reflecting the moonlight. She felt a chill in the air and pulled her coat tighter around her. She wondered how the people of Yalta were coping with the harsh winter and the presence of foreign troops.

The car passed by a few villages, where she could see some lights in the windows and smoke rising from the chimneys. She imagined the lives of the villagers, who had witnessed the German invasion and occupation, and then the Soviet liberation and reoccupation. She wondered if they knew about the historic conference that was taking place in their town, and what they thought of the three leaders who were deciding their fate.

The smell of charred wood and rubber drifted in the air around them. As the faint lights in the distant city grew, so did the scent.

The car reached the outskirts of Yalta, and Erin saw the marks of war. Ares' distinct brand. There were bombed-out buildings, burned-out vehicles, and barbed wire fences. Soviet soldiers were patrolling the streets and had checkpoints at nearly every intersection. She saw posters of Stalin, Roosevelt, and Churchill, with slogans like "Long live the friendship of the peoples!" and "Victory is near!"

The car turned into a driveway, and Erin saw the majestic Livadia Palace, where the conference was being held. The flags of the United States, the United Kingdom, and the Soviet Union were flying over the entrance, and the security guards were standing at attention. There were journalists, diplomats, and military officers milling around the grounds, and the cameras and microphones set up for the press conferences.

Erin felt her blood rush with adrenaline, and her heart pounding inside her chest. It seemed like only a week ago she was just a normal person, sitting in Whitehall Court, going through intelligence reports. Now they had to stop this plot, which it was clear was going to be directed against Churchill and Roosevelt. Losing either of them would be a catastrophe that could change the course of history. She had no idea how they were going to pull this off, but she hoped that they had enough time, and enough luck, to succeed.

Erin steps out of the car, pulling her collar up around her neck, bracing herself in the cold wind. Joey opened the trunk, and everyone began getting their camera cases and press gear.

Her mind was still racing, she looked through the crowd, trying to spot Henry Foster. He had to be stopped, but they also needed to identify Dorothy Smith, his partner. She could only hope they might meet in the throng of bodies outside and she could get a look at her.

Her heartbeat pounded in her ears, nearly, but not quite blocking the quiet sound of her father's watch. There was that clicking. He was releasing the cover and closing it inside his coat pocket. Her nerves began to calm. She looked over at Jasper and he smiled. He had a plan. They might be alright.

THE PALACE WAS A WHITE neoclassical building with a green roof, surrounded by a park and gardens. It had 116 rooms, including a large hall, a dining room, a billiard room, a library, and a cinema.

The palace was divided into three zones. They would go into the left zone where the British were assigned. The Soviets had the central zone, and the Americans were in the right zone.

So far, this part of their job was going smoothly. Their rooms had been prearranged for them and they were at the end of the building with access to the stairs and the exits.

They all gathered in Erin's room and Jasper began to lay out his plan, what little he had put together so far.

"Us men, we will all hit the hallways and see if we can spot Foster. Erin, you and Maeve, stay out of sight for now. He will recognize you right away. We could use the advantage of surprise."

Erin and her mother both agreed, and he went on.

"I'm going to try to get the roster at the front desk. See if we can get a line on any women in Churchill's delegation. I think that is exactly where Dorothy will be."

He looked to his cousin, "I might need a little distraction, if you could come up with something subtle."

"Oh, subtle? Yeah, that is totally my thing. If you just mention subtle Blejack, anyone knows who it is."

"Well, desperate measures for desperate times. I will take whatever I can get." Jasper grinned, "But really, subtle. We don't need a shootout."

"Look, just let Blejack do Blejack. Everything will be fine. You just don't get caught pinching the book. This is only day one, and it won't kick off until 5 p.m." His cousin clasped his hand on his shoulder, "Remember, Jasper, low profile."

Erin and Maeve waited as the men left the room to wander the halls and mingle, working their way into the central section and the far-right section of the building.

It wasn't long before Erin had had enough sitting. She began digging through her things and found some other credentials. She was now going to be part of Churchill's security detail.

"Mom, I can't stand this waiting. I am going to go do my own investigation. I know Foster's face better than any of them."

"I understand. Do you want me to come with you?"

Erin thought for a moment, "No, you better hang back. It might still be to our advantage if he only sees one of us. But I promise, I will be fine. I have some tricks up my sleeves."

Just then her aunt Eris's voice cut in, "I will go with you."

"Holy chicken soup! Where have you been?" Erin turned and wrapped her arms around the mischievous goddess.

"Been busy." She smiled, "There's a war going on, you know."

The three made their reacquaintances and Erin led Eris out the door and down the long hallway. They made their way to the central zone, and Erin showed her papers to the sentry, explaining that she had to make a preliminary inspection before the talks began.

The main conference room was located in the Soviet zone, on the ground floor of the palace. It was a rectangular room with a long wooden table and 35 chairs. The table was covered with a green cloth and had microphones, ashtrays, and nameplates for each delegate. The walls were decorated with portraits of Lenin, Stalin, Roosevelt, and Churchill, as well as maps of Europe and Asia. The room had two large rows of tall arched windows, one facing the sea and the other facing the mountains.

At one end was a large round table. This is where the three leaders and their ranking staff would sit. Her name wouldn't be here, but Erin made a pass around it anyways. Then she turned her attention to the rest of the room.

She walked around the long table, examining the names, looking for Dorothy. At the same time, she looked over the surroundings for any place a person might be hidden. There didn't appear to be any that wouldn't be discovered.

The room was open, with a tall ceiling. There was a fireplace at each end, both with a blaze going. The curtains were all open, letting in the morning light, and they didn't touch the floor. There was no chance of anyone standing behind one and not being seen.

The light reflected off the tall white walls, and it was bright. There were rows of chairs lining each wall and only two doors to the chamber. One to the Russian zone, the other to the American zone.

As she neared the far end of the table, she spotted it. 'Dorothy Smith'. She kept walking, making her mental note and not drawing attention to it.

As she continued, she began looking out the windows. Watching for a spot where she could stand or sit or hide and not be noticed. Someplace she could wait and see the face of the little Nazi wench when she sat down.

She neared the end of the room, back at the doorway and thanked the guard, "Sorry to take up your time, but there will be several of these inspections every day."

"Oh, I am aware," he replied. "There have already been several tours this morning and the sun is barely up."

The guard detail was made up of a mix of American, British and Soviet soldiers, all dressed to the nines. Inspectors got the luck of the draw as to which one would escort them. Or maybe more than one, depending on their mood.

Erin led the invisible Eris back down the hallway and up the stairs to her room, whispering on the way, "I think I have an idea of how to see who this woman is. We need to get my gear and make some adjustments to my appearance and identification."

As they neared the top step, Eris grabbed onto Erin's arm, pulling her back.

"Foster."

Erin squatted down and peeked around the corner. He was just locking his door. She jerked her head back as he turned his head, looking down the hall both ways for anyone that might be watching him.

Erin whispered, "Let's follow him. Maybe we can pick up another lead."

"Good, maybe we can have some fun. This was getting boring."

Erin looked and her with an uncomfortable smile and shook her head "No."

She watched Henry as he turned down the hall going in the opposite direction and entered the stairwell at the other end.

"Come on," she tapped Eris and ran back down the stairs to try to beat Foster to the main floor.

She peeked around the edge of the hallway and waited for him to show. He stepped down the last steps and she pulled her head back, listening carefully for his footsteps. There was noise coming from the main entry area, but she could just make him out.

He paused as he stepped out into the hall, then his steps began to become fainter.

She looked around the corner again just in time to see him turn toward the main door.

She gave Eris a light tap on the arm and quickly went through the doorway to her left and outside.

There was a garden with hedges a short distance away and she walked across the short span of grass to get behind the greenery.

Foster emerged just as she was able to slip down below the top of the bushy plants. She could still see him there, and he was walking toward the cars, parked at the edge of the broad drive.

She began to move along behind the row of leaves toward the cars, watching him and staying out of sight.

He stopped at a car about three quarters of the way down the line.

"He is leaving. We need to get to the car." Erin said quietly. "I want to know where he is going."

"Finally." Eris sighed, "Something I can do."

She put her hand on Erin's arm, and they appeared squatted down by the staff car she had arrived in.

"Glad I wasn't standing up for everyone to see me appear out of nowhere." Erin gave her aunt a light punch. "We need some boundaries, you and me. No zapping me through space without a warning."

"Look how sassy you are getting. Barely over a week and you are making rules."

They climbed into the car and Erin began looking for the keys. Ashtray, visor, glove box, under the seat...

Foster's car pulled out into the roadway and began to leave, stopping at the checkpoint.

Erin was having no luck. No keys.

"May I?" Eris asked.

Erin stopped her search and looked at her, "Ok, fine."

Eris put her arm around her niece, and they reappeared outside the large grounds, on the other side of the road behind some trees.

"That wasn't so bad, was it?" Eris tilted her head like a little puppy and smiled.

"To be honest, it is still unsettling. My head is spinning every time you do that."

"Let's hope he isn't going too far then. This is going to get bumpy for you."

The black car pulled away from the sentries and started down the road. Eris and Erin watched until he was nearly out of sight, then Eris did her thing, and they were caught up again.

Eris repeated this until the man pulled into a parking lot in front of a large hotel.

The name was written in Russian, but it was the Hotel Bristol, which was built in 1902. Erin had been here before, several years ago, before the war started. It was a three-story building with a U-shaped layout, facing the sea. There was a large courtyard with a fountain and a garden. The facade is made of yellow brick and white stucco, with arched windows and balconies. The roof was tiled in red and there was a tower in the center.

He stepped out of the car and put on a low brimmed hat that matched his dark suit, then walked down the sidewalk to a door that led to a stairwell.

Erin was ducking behind a car, watching him as he went up the stairs, then reappearing on the second level walkway that went around the inside of the building. He stopped at a door and gave it a few light taps and someone inside opened it, letting him inside.

Now Erin had to wonder who was on the other side of that door too and she said as much to Eris.

"Now that is something I can take care of. Sit tight little sis."

"Aunt." Erin corrected.

"Shut up. I'll be back."

Eris disappeared and Erin sat, squatted next to the car, looking into her bag like she was doing something.

Several minutes later the man reemerged from the doorway. He was carrying a small brown satchel. Similar to a briefcase, but open at the top. It had a pair of rounded leather wrapped handles and a small strap with a button that closed over the top.

The door closed behind him, and he opened the satchel, looking inside it.

At the same time Eris popped in behind Erin, startling her. She jerked and looked at her aunt just as a gunshot echoed across the courtyard.

Eris let out a yelp like a puppy who had just been stepped on. Erin turned back to see Foster trying to aim at her and she dropped to the ground.

Eris had been clipped by the bullet across her upper arm, and she was bleeding.

"What the...? you can be shot?"

Eris answers her, "Well yeah, we aren't invincible. Imagine how arrogant Gods would be if that were the case."

"Don't you think that is something that maybe you should have mentioned before?"

"Been busy..." Eris grins and wraps her arm with a piece of her tunic that she cut loose.

Foster let off a couple more shots, ricocheting off the ground near them.

"Are you ok?" she asked the damaged goddess.

"Well, you are going to need to give me a minute here. This really hurts."

"Take your time. But I am done with this guy."

Erin disregarded any thoughts of witnesses and turned on her charm. Her eyes became small infernos of indigo, and her arms began to boil with sparks.

She stood and spun around at once, throwing her hands out extended together and a long tight bolt of electricity shot straight through the nazi agent.

She sat down and turned off her fireworks, leaned over and took the ends of Eris's improvised bandage and finished wrapping her wound, tying it directly over the spot that was bleeding to put more pressure on it.

"I have to be honest. I think this is nonsense. What kind of gods can be shot and wounded?"

"Umm, this kind. Me. Do you even read? Ever heard of the Iliad?"

"How's that feel?" Erin asked her with a bit more empathy.

"I'll be honest with you too. It hurts like hell." Eris leaned back against the car and closed her eyes for a minute. "I can get you back to the room. But I think we might be on foot for a while after that."

She drew a deep breath and put her hand around Erin's arm.

MATTY WAITED IN THE plane for Blejack, Erin and the rest to return from the conference. She had curled up on a bench at the side of the fuselage and was finally getting to have some sleep.

But she woke with a start when she heard footsteps ringing from the metal steps that were set against her plane.

Outside, was one of the men who had been on the plane behind them or someone they knew. She didn't even think about them knowing her plane or being a threat anymore.

She cursed herself for getting sloppy. Letting her guard down.

She jumped up quietly and reached behind her seat, getting out a small carbine with a long wooden stock. She moved silently past the door and stood to the rear of it, expecting the man to look to the cockpit first, she might get the jump on him.

She could hear the man turning the handle and the bolt sliding, releasing the door from its frame. She held her breath.

He carefully swung the door out, trying not to make a sound.

The light reflected off the metal on the inside of the door and the man's silhouette began to intrude into her space.

She pulled the rifle back and laid the butt of it into the side of his head.

He fell to the floor and rolled, grabbing his head, he pointed back up at her with a pistol.

She tried to dodge to the side and slammed the butt toward his face and a shot went off with a tiny 'piff'.

Matty fell back and grabbed her side.

She landed with her seat on the bench and a wave of coldness went through her.

She told herself to stay focused. Stop the bleeding. Get the door closed and take care of this guy.

She looked around for something she could wad up against the bullet hole in her flesh and her eyes settled on the duffle bag that Erin had used as a pillow.

She forced herself onto her feet and crouched over, stumbling across the plane to the other bench.

With one hand she released the spring clip that held the little link through the eyelets, keeping the bags contents safely inside. She reached in and grabbed whatever came first, in this case, a shirt.

"Ah man, I liked that shirt." She gave it one last look, then pulled the one she was wearing away from her wound and stuffed it into place.

She held her right forearm against the lump of cloth and wet blood, taking another breath. Then she pulled off her belt and wrapped it around the improvised bandage.

Matty felt her leg going numb and tingling. She sat there and looked at the man on the floor. She pulled her small rifle up under her right arm, above the wound, and kept it pointed toward him with her other hand.

"I hope you are already dead. Freaking Nazi piece of crap. But I don't mind killing you twice."

MAEVE SAT ON THE BED and rubbed some ointment onto Eris's wound, a long shallow gash across her upper arm. She had given it a good cleaning and was now wrapping it with some clean gauze.

"I think this will heal up fine for you, sis. How in the world did he manage to get a bead on you?"

"He just got lucky. He was firing at Erin when I popped in and distracted her. She moved and I got the bullet instead."

"Well, it sounds like Erin got lucky too. I am glad this is no worse than it is. She is lucky to have you watching her back." Maeve taped off the wrap.

"I didn't try to get shot on purpose. It was just dumb luck."

"Well, you both will be okay. That is good enough for me. I will look at that again tomorrow for you. Just leave it covered."

"You know, Maeve, I do have a regular doctor." She smiled, "Paean will make this just like new."

"But does he have my soft bedside manner?"

"I don't think he has any manner at all, now that I think about it."

"Well, there you go. You will be fine." Maeve starts putting her supplies away.

Erin had been watching the two carry on, chomping at the bit to find out what Eris had learned inside that room.

"Eris? What did you learn in the room? I went and killed our last lead because he shot you."

"Oh yeah. That. They aren't waiting for the conference. Dorothy is going to do it at lunch."

Erin furled her brow and looked at her watch. "Oh my god, Eris! It is eleven now. Where is the lunch?"

"No idea. Just that Dorothy is going to be there and make her move on Roosevelt and Churchill. With them out of the way, Stalin will dump the allies and go it alone, trying to take more territory for himself. Britain and America will turn on him and Germany will have time to recover and go on the offensive again."

Erin bolted for the door, unlatching it to go and see if she could find out where the lunch was taking place.

Just as she did, the door opened and Jasper and Blejack were standing in front of her.

"Dad, any idea where Churchill is having lunch today?"

"Matter of fact, I do." he answered. "Right here in the building. They have a meeting room where they are really hashing out the details."

Erin let out a small sigh of relief. "I need to be there. Smith is going to make her move there. And we had better get everyone ready to move out. If this goes wrong, it is going to go really wrong."

"You can't go alone, I will..."

"No, you need to get the car outside past the guards and on the road. If I have to stop her the hard way, she is part of the British delegation. They are going to see me as the bad guy here. Besides, she is going to help me."

Erin pointed her thumb at Eris with her bandaged arm.

"Oh hi, Eris. Didn't even notice you there. Something happen to your arm?" Jasper asked as though he didn't know.

"Ever the barrel of monkeys, you are, Jasper. You know something happened to my arm. I was out taking bullets for Erin. What were you doing? Sneaking around the palace and pinching things that don't belong to you?"

"That is a pretty fair summary. Yeah, pretty much that."

Jasper walked to the window and waved Erin over, "Here," he pointed down to the main floor, "Right inside there. They are probably there now talking and filling the room with cigar smoke."

"Are you ready Eris?" she asked, still looking down at the room.

"Yes, I am fine now. But I am going to go get this fixed up soon."

"Thank you." She turned back to Eris, "For saving me from a bullet in my head too."

“That’s what aunts do.” Eris blessed her with her creepy grin.

As a rule, Eris’s aunting skills were not really the ones you would want applied to your average daughter or son. But she was the right aunt for this job and this niece.

Erin picked up her camera bag and a tripod and led Eris down the stairs again. Jasper, Blejack and Maeve got busy gathering Paul and Joey back to the room and packing up.

Erin stopped in the lawn and set the tripod up, attaching the camera to the top, then another segment to the side of the camera. It was a magnifying lens. It worked like a telescope or binoculars but was less conspicuous. And it could be explained away as a tool to match the telephoto lens. It allowed her to see what the camera saw, giving her a clear photograph.

She dialed it in so she could see inside the windows and the three leaders at the table. She squatted down and looked through the view lense as though she was studying for a shot.

What she saw sent her heart racing again.

Dorothy was standing beside and slightly behind Roosevelt. Her hand was on his shoulder. He was turned in his seat looking up at her with his own hand on her wrist.

He was smiling as she seemed to be speaking to him.

Then Erin saw something else. A large ring on her finger. Like a high school class ring. Too large for a young girl to be wearing around.

“Crap!” she let out. “That witch!”

Erin focused her thoughts on the young woman's arm, and she jerked it away from the President’s shoulder.

Dorothy put her other hand on the arm that had just gone paralyzed and decided to excuse herself from the conversation.

“Oh, she doesn’t get off that easy,” Eris said, seeming somewhat disappointed with Erin’s mild punishment.

She disappeared and Erin watched her reappear inside the room, leaning over to Dorothy’s ear.

The lady spy walked for the door to the courtyard and Erin picked up her camera and tripod, heading to cut her off.

When she stepped outside, she started to go through her purse. She found a small metallic box and opened it. Inside was what looked like a large cigarette lighter. She unfolded it and started to put it to her head.

Just as she was going to pull the trigger, she saw Erin. Seeing the SIS officer with her wavy red hair was enough to bring her out of Eris’s hypnosis for a moment and she pointed her tiny gun toward Erin.

Erin ducked and held her camera in front of her as the tiny weapon made its popping sound.

Without even thinking, Erin pulled out her own pistol, this one not a toy.

Three shots in quick succession and the Nazi spy was on the ground.

“Well, it went bad, Erin.” Eris confirmed for her.

“Shit!”

“Time for fun. I can’t zap you now. People are watching. Run baby girl. I will make sure you get to the road.”

Guards were running from the building and from the station at the end of the drive.

Erin gave her camera a last look, then began to run toward the road and the car.

Men were yelling behind her, “Stop! Stop or I’ll fire!”

They did fire, and she ran. Eris moved like a gust of wind from one soldier to the next, shifting their aim, whispering sweet nothings, anything she felt would keep their bullets away from Erin.

Erin made it to the car and the door was open waiting for her. She jumped into the back seat and Jasper put his foot down.

Eris smiled and looked at her arm again. "She will probably be fine for a while." And she was gone again.

MATTY HEARS A FAMILIAR voice on the radio, "Matty! Get the plane started, we have to leave now!"

She pulls herself together and pushes the limp man's body under the other bench with her legs. She bites down and the pain pours through her body. She leans forward, using her rifle as a crutch and makes it to the cockpit.

She slides down into her seat and fires off the engines. "Seriously, what in the H E double toothpicks have they got me into?"

As she pulls her safety belts around her waist, she sees some other cars racing toward her plane, attempting to block it off. She revs the engines and starts the plane rolling, dropping the rear door.

She tells them on the radio, "We gotta go now guys or we never go. Put your foot down."

Jasper is driving down the runway chasing after the plane with his foot to the floor.

Shots rang past them from the cars behind.

He lines up on the cargo door that is dragging an inch from the ground and guns the engine.

The car hits the ramp and makes it nearly on then the plane pulls away, dropping the car's front wheels back to the pavement.

The car jerks and swerves a moment and Jasper brings it back in line. He hit the gas hard again.

The front tires hit the ramp and gave them a bounce and then the rear tires hit it. For a moment they spun against the edge of the door, then grabbed and the car jerked forward onto the rear of the plane.

Jasper hit the brakes and the car lurched to a stop with all four wheels rubbing the benches on either side.

Matty yelled for Blejack, and he rushed into the cockpit. "Help me pull the yoke."

Blejack makes it to the copilot seat, and she barks orders to him as she continues to pull levers and twist knobs. She pulls on the throttle and sets the plane into motion.

Matty checked the fuel gauge and frowned. "I'm running low on gas, and we still have a long way to go."

Then she fell limp in her seat, leaning to her side, exposing the trail of blood down her right side. She heard Blejack yell for Maeve and she passed out.

Chapter 11: The Fallout

Someplace over the Black Sea.
February 4, 1945

MATTY WAS LAYING ON the floor on top of everything they could find to make her a pad. Maeve was sitting down on the floor, looking at her wound.

"We have to get the bullet out and stop this bleeding. Find me anything. Anything I can reach in with to get hold of it." Maeve pleaded.

"There is nothing. We have been through everything. Just the dirty tools we used fixing the plane." Erin told her.

Poor Matty was soaked in her own blood from her midsection down to her ankle. Maeve was holding a thick cloth over the hole that was still leaking her life away.

"Erin, you need to try with your power. Control it. Pull the bullet out and cauterize the bleeding."

"Mom, I can move trees, but this? I don't think I can do this. It will get away from me and she will die."

"I will help you. We have to try, or she is going to die anyways."

"I don't want to kill her. This is crazy." Erin just stared at Matty. She liked Matty. They had been friends since they first met on her first mission in the field.

Maeve took Erin's hand. "I will help you. We are going to save her. I felt the same way the first time I was thrown into trying to save a life. You just have to do what you can."

Erin held her hand out in front of her, forming her index finger and thumb into a pinching shape, and lit her blue flames.

The blue charge glowed around her arms. Maeve talked to her, soothing her.

"Bring it down a little. Then focus on the bullet inside her. I have some things I can do too."

Erin kneeled by her mom, focusing on the wound, searching for the bullet.

"You find it and I will keep her safe."

Erin glanced her eyes at her mom then went back to Matty.

The blue bolts found their way into the open hole in Matty's waist and Maeve put her hands around the wound.

Somehow, she contained Erin's power into the one spot, and Erin took hold of the small lead round. She pulled her hands away, bringing the bullet with her.

Her skin swelled around the hole, and more blood began to stream out. Then the bullet fell to the floor and the bleeding had stopped.

Maeve got into her bag and pulled out her medical supplies. Rinsed the wound with alcohol, then wadded up some gauze and packed it.

Erin watched, “She is going to be glad she slept through this part.”

“You guys, help us lift her.” Maeve called over to Jasper and the men.

Paul stepped over everyone and took her arms at the shoulder, lifting her forward.

Maeve and Erin passed a broad linen wrap around her, over the gauze and tied it off.

Paul gently laid her back down on the pile of clothes and blankets.

“What do you think?” Jasper asked.

Maeve looked up at him, her eyes tired, “She lost a lot of blood.” She looked back down at the pale blonde. “She was bleeding a long time before we got back.”

Maeve noticed the man under the bench.

“Oh! That’s new.” She pointed to him.

“Well, we can guess where the bullet came from now. Paul, want to help me dig him out of there and drag him to the back? We can go through his pockets and see if we can find out who he is.”

“Give me his coat when you do. She needs to be kept warm. And then you guys go hide behind the car and let me get her cleaned up.”

ERIN WENT UP FRONT to check on Blejack. She stood behind him and hugged him, “How are you doing uncle Bleej?”

“I am getting the hang of it. Is she okay?”

“We got the bullet out and stopped the bleeding. We just have to wait now.”

He didn’t say anything. He just kept looking forward out the windshield. They had just crossed a span of open water and he hoped they were aimed back at the last fuel stop Matty had made.

“Keep your spirits up. She has the best doctor around for miles.”

“You know we are miles from anything, right?”

“Yeah, but it would be the same if we were downtown London.”

“Yeah, you’re right. Maeve will do anything she can to save her.”

“I’ll be right back. I need to clean her seat up for her.”

Erin went back and gathered some of the clothes that were already a mess and the alcohol bottle from her mom. Then she returned to join Blejack in the cockpit and started wiping down the pilot’s seat.

As she knelt down by the seat, she began to hear a strange crackling sound. She stopped to listen and could make out what sounded like a voice occasionally.

“Blejack, what is that sound?”

He took his eyes off the clouds and the distant ground below and looked down at her. He could hear it now too. He looked down at his pocket and pulled out the small radio and held it to his ear.

"It's coming from this. I forgot I even had it. I don't think any of us ever used them."

He handed it to Erin, and she placed it next to her own ear.

"Just push the speaker, right?"

"Yes, but that takes us to our own frequency. Before you do that, just try to tune the dial and see if you can bring the signal in."

Erin sat down in the pilot's seat and began to turn the dial slowly with her thumb. She eased it up and then down and back until she was getting what almost amounted to a signal.

Now she could make out words. They faded in and out, and they were in German.

"Aren't we a little far behind the Soviet lines to be picking up German?" She asked her uncle.

"I think so, not that I really know where we are."

When they had taken off, Matty had set the heading to the West, and slightly north. Blejack just kept the yoke going in the same path with no idea where they were headed or if he needed to adjust anything. He just trusted that Matty would have set him up before she passed out. It was a leap of faith, but he needed that right now. He wanted to believe that she was just having a setback and she would be back in her seat any minute.

There was a mountain range in the distance ahead and he was getting concerned. It was going to be beyond his skill to land this thing on a runway or in a field. If they were to run out of fuel over those mountains, he was pretty sure it was going to turn into that 'crash and burn' scenario he had warned about earlier.

He glanced back to the fuel gauge, and it had somehow not managed to move upwards anymore. He wondered if there was enough vacuum on the tanks now that they would collapse when he dropped in altitude and the air pressure increased.

"The signal is getting clearer, Blejack. I think we are close to them."

Erin leaned up toward the glass, watching below for any signs of where the signal might be coming from.

Blejack didn't think he had let the plane drop any, but the ground was moving closer. He was approaching the lower slopes of the range.

"Blejack, there! In the trees, do you see it?" She pointed excitedly.

"Yes, I think so. Is that an antenna mast with branches on it?"

"Yes. And in the trees behind, there is some kind of platform. I think it is a missile platform. Turn off to the south and find someplace to land! We need to know what is going on in there."

Blejack got cold chill, "Crap. Go tell everyone to strap everything down and come back and help me. I have never landed before. I only hope I can remember everything she did when we landed in the field."

Just then one of the engines started to go out of phase. Blejack looked out his window and saw the propeller was beginning to show itself every few seconds.

"Okay, well, it just got worse. Just yell at them and strap in, Erin."

Erin ran to the back of the plane and shouted to the others, "We have to land now! Strap everything down and get ready for a bumpy ride!"

She could see the worried faces of Maeve and Jasper who were still tending to Matty. Matty was still on the floor, wrapped in the unknown man's coat. Her skin was pale, but Maeve had gotten her into clean clothes. She made a silent wish that Matty would make it through this.

Paul got down on the floor and put his weight over Matty's torso, "Strap in you two," indicating Jasper and Maeve, "Put your feet on me and try to keep us from flying through the cabin."

They both climbed on the bench behind them and did as Paul asked. Stretching their legs in front of themselves, they tried to anchor the big man to the floor on top of their friend.

Joey ran with a limp up through the center of the plane from the rear carrying a ratchet strap and tossed the hook end to Jasper.

"Catch that on the rail under the seat." he pointed beneath the bench they were seated on.

He spun the strap out of its roll and hooked the other end to the opposite side, pulling it through the ratchet mechanism with a loud zipping sound.

As he rapidly cranked it snug, Paul barked at him, "Not too tight there. Still got ribs and organs inside."

Joey dropped onto the seat behind himself and pulled the belts around his waist and shoulders, clamping himself in place.

Erin turned back to the front of the plane and quickly strapped herself into a seat next to Blejack and looked out of the window. She saw the mountains looming closer, and the trees below. The green of grassy knolls and pastures had given way to banks of snow and black boulders. She wondered where Blejack was going to find a place to land. She began to wonder if they would survive the landing.

Blejack's voice cut through her thoughts, "Erin, I think I see a clearing ahead, but it's not very big. I'm going to try to land there, but it's going to be tight. Hold on to something."

She grabbed the armrests of her seat and felt the plane tilt to the left. The clearing came into view, a patch of snowy field with clumps of grass surrounded by trees and rocks. She saw the plane's shadow on the ground, getting bigger and bigger. She heard the engines roar, and the hydraulics dropping their wheels.

"What am I missing!" Blejack yelled at himself, frustrated with all of the dials and buttons and switches.

The plane touched the ground and bounced up again. It hit the ground again, harder, and skidded forward. Erin felt the plane shake and rattle and heard the metal scrape and crunch.

The plane began to slide sideways over the snow-covered ground with a loud thrashing sound.

The trees and rocks rushed past the front window. They pushed themselves back into their seats, hoping that none of them would hit the plane.

The smell of smoke and fuel began to drift into the cockpit. She hoped that the plane wouldn't catch fire as the cold air pushed the smell of the engines into the compartment.

The plane slowed down and came to a stop. Erin felt a jolt and heard a thud as the fuselage rolled toward her side of the plane, resting on the wing. She pushed herself away from the wall and looked out the window and saw the propeller on the right engine spin off into the air and land on a grassy spot, stabbing one blade into the dirt then tipping over onto another.

"Flaps!" Blejack slapped his hand on the yoke.

Erin looked toward Blejack, thinking it was a good thing the prop didn't come toward them.

Blejack had seen it too, "I think we can fix that." He smiled at her.

They both paused, basking in the thought that they were still alive.

"Any landing is a good landing?" Blejack asked.

He reached forward and flipped a switch, "Maybe we can get the car out, if it didn't roll over back there."

"Wait!" Erin tried to get out but the big door at the rear began dropping.

There was a loud groaning sound and a slight feeling of weightlessness as the airplane began to rock. Then she felt her seat lifting her as the plane dropped back to Blejack's side.

Next there was a huge thud and more sounds of metallic moaning, as the body of the plane adjusted itself to its new seating arrangement.

"Never mind." Erin sat still and waited for whatever was coming next.

She let out a huge sigh, "Let's go check on everyone else."

They both unstrapped and moved out of the cockpit into the cargo bay.

The cold air was filling the rear of the long aluminum tube from the huge open door at the rear. But it looked like they had kept the ship in one piece.

Paul was still pinning Matty down to the floor and the other three were untying themselves from their restraints.

"You guys hurry every chance you get. I think Joey snapped my spine with his strap." Paul grumbled at them.

Joey squatted down and gave the ratchet an extra click or two before releasing his giant friend.

"Hey! Don't think I didn't notice that."

Paul rolled off of Matty, who seemed the same as she was before the graceful dance that Blejack had just performed with the C-47.

"You need to go find you a treetop to sit in and remember your position."

Joey grinned, "Not me. My crow's nest days are behind me."

Paul put his ear next to Matty's face, listening to make sure she was still with them. Then he turned his head to Blejack, "Hate to pressure you, but we need to get that pneumonia hole shut back there."

"That's no joke, "Jasper chimed in to support Paul's cause.

"Get your big butt up off that girl and help me get the car down the ramp and I will close it up."

Blejack stepped around Paul and headed toward the car. Joey followed him, and they began unshackling the sedan.

The crates that the car had its wheels parked against were now wedged against them. Blejack grabbed a rusty crowbar from the tool locker and went to work freeing them, as the frigid wind cut through his face and hands.

Joey climbed into the driver's seat and cranked the starter, pushing the smell of raw gasoline and burnt oil into their abode as the engine sprang to life.

Blejack leaned on the driver's door and tapped the glass, looking at Joey sitting behind the wheel. "Just keep the car straight and get some speed before you hit the ground. Don't get it stuck on the ramp." He said, as he cranked the window down a few inches.

Joey checked over his shoulder and nodded that he understood.

He began backing up, adjusting slightly the first few feet, then revved the engine, shoving the axle against another wooden box.

Blejack waved his hands, "Stop, let me get it out."

He went to the back of the car and pried the cracked wooden box out from under the rear end. The bar made a loud clang as he tossed it to the side and dragged the narrow package out of the way.

The witch-doctor pulled his collar close around his neck and face, giving the path a last look for any other impediments. He slapped his hand on the deck lid and walked around the side of the car.

"Go! Give it hell."

Joey looked back over his shoulder again and mashed on the throttle.

The car made loud double clanking noises as it went over the edge of the door that doubled as a ramp. He gunned it just a little bit more down the short grade, sending him out the rear and into the snowy field behind.

"Go, go, go!" Blejack yelled, as he ran after the car. He put his grip on the nose of the grill and pushed, as the tires wailed and began to spin.

Joey tried to turn the front wheels, but they were packed with snow now. The rear tires began to sink deeper as they heated up, melting into the bank.

"Damn it, damn it, damn it!" Joey cursed, as he furiously pounded the steering wheel. "We're not going anywhere!"

"Kill it and let's get the cargo door shut. We can dig this mess out later."

Joey checked over the gauges, noting there was plenty of fuel. He shut the car off and they walked back up the ramp.

Blejack hit a button at the top of the landing and the big door groaned and squealed, lifting itself back into place and sealing the cold wind outside.

Maeve had a worried look on her face. She was holding Matty's head in her lap. "She's too cold. We have to get her warmer."

"I can start the car and turn the heat on. If we can get her out there." Joey offered.

"Yes, let's do that." Maeve ran her palm over the sleeping woman's brow.

"Help me find a shovel or something to dig with, Joey. We need to clear the exhaust or that will do her in before anything else." Paul opened the tool locker, scrounging around inside.

Joey and Blejack both began looking around the cargo bay for anything they could use. Paul found a folding trench shovel in the locker. It was only about two feet long. On one end there was a shovel head and a pick tooth. They folded down onto the handle when not in use so you could carry it easily. When you needed it, you folded it out and there was a threaded ring that locked the head in place.

"One down."

Joey looked over at Paul and stuck his thumbs up in the air. He spotted the crate he had tried to run over and some of the boards had been broken. He took hold at one of the breaks and pulled the board loose from the box. He held it out, handing it to Blejack and then got a second for himself.

Now that the crate was open, he brushed away some shredded paper and sawdust, exposing rifle barrels.

"Those might come in handy too."

"I'll see if we have any ammo when we get her taken care of." Blejack aimed his board toward Matty.

Joey picked up the ladder they had used earlier, and the three men opened the side door and lowered themselves out of the plane, closing it up behind them.

For a half hour that seemed like four, they dug around the car and stomped down a wide path to the rear of the plane to carry Matty.

The big door dropped again, and they rushed her out to the back seat. Maeve sat inside and held her head up on her lap. They folded her legs down onto the floor and covered her with coats and clothes and the few blankets that they found inside the C-47.

They all got in front and warmed themselves from the cutting wind.

"I saw a cabin as we came down. I don't think it is far from here." He pointed back toward the long skid marks the plane had cut through the snow. "When my blood thaws, I will make a trek out and see if I can find it. Maybe it's empty and we can relocate there."

Jasper opened the door and got out, letting Joey in for his turn at the heater. "I'll go with you. Come get me on the plane.

I am going to see if I can find that man's pistol at least. Maybe some ammo for them rifles."

THEY SMASHED THEIR boots through the snow along the narrow roadway for twenty minutes. It was only a few inches deep and it looked undisturbed.

Then the trees opened up on the left to a small log cabin. Its roof was covered with snow over wooden shingles. It sloped down on all four sides with a half gable above on two ends.

There was a small porch at the front that went the width of the house. The roof was held up on each end by cedar logs with their bark shaved away. There was a small pile of firewood at one end. Some small empty wooden boxes, a few broken metal tools, remnants of an old dress. Around the base were bundles of straw, closing off the cold air.

The snow hadn't been broken by footsteps in some time. The driveway was meant for mules and not cars. They were definitely alone here.

They stepped past the falling split rail fence and looked around the humble home. There was a small outbuilding in the rear, near the tree line and an old well that had a good level of water.

They carefully made the climb up the steps built from a mix of slabs of stone and hand-hewn timbers to the front door. Blejack pulled the rudimentary wooden latch and called inside.

"Hello?"

It was no surprise. There was no answer. The place had been abandoned for a long time.

They went through the door, and it was just as small on the inside as it was on the outside. There was a small sofa to the left and an old dresser. On the right was a bed and a door into the next room. In the center was a potbelly wood stove.

Straight ahead was an open doorway into the kitchen. It was as simple as they come. A small counter with a sink basin, a few shelves and a table with four chairs. Another door to the left went to a mud room or pantry, whichever you prefer to call it.

The door in the main room led into a long bedroom that ran the length of the cabin. There were two full size beds in here and another old dresser.

"This will work," Jasper was happy for their find.

"Be a nice change from those hard benches." Blejack agreed.

"You want to start a fire here and I will trudge back and get the rest of them moving this way?"

Blejack didn't mind that at all. "You have yourself a deal. It'll be nice and toasty when you get back."

"Just so you don't overheat, look around and gather us more wood while I am gone. Be nice to keep a fire all night."

"Hah! Always a catch." Blejack opened the stove to inspect the inside, "No problem. I'll have us all set."

BY THE TIME THAT JASPER returned to the others, Paul and Joey had helped Erin get the car across the field and nearly to the road. They had used more of the lumber from the crates in the plane to give the tires traction, then pushed and dug until they had it sitting at the gate.

"I guess I could have stayed back there with Blejack." He could see the exertion on both the men's faces.

"We didn't want to wait until we lost all the daylight." Paul answered. The sun had gone before Jasper left the cabin.

"Joey did a hell of a job." Jasper had to pull on Paul's chain just a little.

"Thanks, Cappy. It wasn't my usual task, but I just kept my head down. Before I knew it, I had the car over here. When I looked up, Paul was already here too, leaning on the back of the car."

"Oh, so it's going to be both of you now." Paul reached down below the bumper and got himself a handful of the white powder. He stood there looking at both of them, packing it into a tight ball.

"So, it's on, is it?" Jasper grinned.

Paul let it sail, and Jasper took it on the shoulder, sending nice cold fragments down his collar.

"Oh! Nice hit." He ducked behind the sedan and gathered his own ammo. Both Joey and Paul disappeared beneath the window line, arming themselves.

Seconds later there was a rain of snowballs passing over the car, men laughing and taunting each other.

Erin sat behind the wheel, shaking her head with a big smile on her face.

"How long should we let them go at this, mom?" she asked Maeve.

"Better let them get it out of their systems. Otherwise, they won't go to bed tonight and they will keep us up."

Erin let them play for several minutes then their shots started hitting the car more frequently, making a loud thudding sound.

"Ok, kids. Dying girl in the car. Remember?"

They all stopped and laughed at each other. Jasper shoved Paul's shoulder as they walked to the car. Then Paul grabbed Jasper by the waist and lifted him into the air. He ran a few feet and tossed him into a snowbank.

Jasper began to laugh again. "Damn it, Paul. My clothes are full of snow."

"It won't melt nothing."

They fussed around, trying to fit everyone into the car. Paul and Jasper managed to squeeze into the front with Erin and Joey finally lifted Matty's legs and slid under.

"Good thing she isn't any taller." Joey remarked.

"Well, you just sit tight back there and keep her out of the floor. Paul and I will do any unstucking we need to do on the way. Besides, you could probably use a rest from carrying the car across that field" Jasper leaned his head forward trying not to laugh. Paul gave him a blast with his elbow into the ribs.

Through a combination of the extra weight in the car and luck, it only took Erin a few minutes to make the drive to the cabin. She went past the 'driveway' and backed the car in. The trail went uphill to the cabin and had a deep rut in the center where the rain had washed it out over the years.

Everyone got out and smelled the pine smoke coming from the stone chimney coming up and out of the center of the roof. Paul unlocked the trunk and he and Joey gathered up the rifles and ammo they had collected to take them inside.

Jasper, Maeve and Erin lifted Matty from the car and carried her to the bed in the main room. They covered her and tucked her in, propping her head up on a pillow.

Once they were satisfied that she was going to be as restful as she could be, Maeve and Erin began to look around. They checked the cupboards and found a few things. Flour, starch, some canned vegetables that appeared to be edible.

Erin looked into the pantry and found a warm looking coat hanging on a nail. She pulled it down, thinking this might be an improvement. She began to dust off the shoulders and turned it over to see a six-pointed star sewn on the breast.

Her stomach turned, thinking of what happened to the people whose home they were inside of now. She folded it over her arm and stepped back into the kitchen.

"Dad," she held it up for him.

He looked at her and shook his head sadly.

They all knew the people who built this cabin were probably all murdered by the Nazis and gone now.

Erin carefully folded the coat and placed it onto the dresser in the living area. All the happiness that had been built up with Jasper and the boys playing in the snow and finding a warm place to rest had dissolved in just a few seconds.

"Nobody takes anything from here." she said looking down at it. "Only what food we need."

Chapter 12: Swan Song

Near Bacau, Romania.
February 5, 1945

EVERYONE WOKE TO BOOTS stomping into the pantry. Blejack strolled into the kitchen with an armload of potatoes and some other canned foods. He put them down on the counter and the potatoes cascaded out of his arms like a small avalanche.

Erin and Maeve had both slept in the same bed as Matty in the living room. Now they were sitting and leaning up.

"Can you be any louder?" Erin squeezed the words out of her still sleeping voice box.

"I think I did pretty good. But I could dig a little deeper if you need it." He stuck his head through the door. "Good morning. I made coffee and found a root cellar."

She flopped back down, refusing to climb out from under the warmth of the blankets. "I just need a week's sleep. That's all I want."

"Sleep when you're dead. We got living to do." He went back into the kitchen and began digging around for a paring knife.

"Oh..." she growled, "Then you must be tired."

He ignored her, finding the knife he had hoped for. He sat down in a chair next to the wash basin and started shaving the potatoes.

Maeve got up and checked the fire. It looked like the witch-doctor had already loaded it up. But nothing warmer than standing in front of the open door of a potbellied stove.

Erin rolled over and pulled the blanket over her head and fell back to sleep.

Her mom joined Blejack in the kitchen. He peeled away, making a nice pile of potato skins in the basin.

"What's the plan?" she asked him.

"Hash browns. I found some sorghum too. Hash browns with sorghum on them. That is the best."

She picked up a pan and a grater that he had on the table and sat down next to him.

"How about some help then?"

"Have at it. Many hands make a light load."

He passed her a few peeled spuds, and she began shredding them into long slivers.

Soon the small cabin was filled with the smell of fried potatoes and coffee. Jasper and Paul were first to reach the kitchen, both crowding in on the fresh pot of joe.

Blejack had been busy. There was a bowl of sugar and a teaspoon all set for Jasper. He dropped in his required two teaspoons and brought the life-giving elixir to his lips.

In the other room there was another welcome sound. Matty's voice. Erin lifted the blanket and looked into her eyes, only inches away. Not sure if she was happy to see her alive, or if she should kill her and go back to sleep.

She decided to take one for the team and be happy for Matty this time.

"Just stay in bed for a minute. Let me get you some water." She pushed Matty softly back onto her pillow.

She got up and went to the kitchen. Blejack had a fresh pitcher sitting on the counter. She looked into the cabinet and got a cup, gave it a quick rinse and filled it for the recovering blonde in the other room.

"Mind if we swap places, Erin?" Blejack asked.

"Oh, I guess I can this time."

He handed her his knife and got up, wiping his hands on a small towel.

He took the water to Matty who warmed him with her smile.

"Can you sit?" he asked her.

"Might need just a little help this time."

"No problem." He sat the cup down and lifted her up. "If you are up to it, use your feet to push back and I will set you against the headboard."

"Let's try it." She closed her eyes, hoping the pain would be less than she expected.

Blejack slipped a couple more pillows behind her then lifted her below her arms as she pushed with her legs.

"That's enough." she furled her brow. "No more."

"Okay. I'm not going to move you anymore. When you are ready, I have your water."

She used her hand to put a small amount of pressure on the bandage over her gunshot. She gave a little gasp. "What the hell did you all get me into?"

He stroked her hair gingerly. "I want you to try to remember, my plan was to dart you and leave you in Paris."

She jerked her eyes open and punched him in the chest, hurting herself more than it did him.

"You asshole!"

He laughed and then she did too.

"The good news is that it is all over. Well, maybe you can't go to Crimea anymore. And your plane might not be how you left it with me. But things are looking up."

"Oh, they are, are they?"

"Well, there is one other thing."

She stopped smiling again. "And?"

"We accidentally found a nazi missile base and we want to go blow it up."

"Jesus Christ you guys! Can we ever just spend one day together where I am not being shot at or someone trying to blow me up or crash my plane?"

She looked back at him, "And what about my plane?"

"I really can't say. I am not a pilot, you know. But it didn't look the same after I landed."

"Do you have any idea how hard it is for a woman to get a C-47 from the military?"

"You have to give me credit, I flew it as long as I could before trying to land. One engine had already run out when I decided it was time." he paused for a second, "And I am pretty sure they didn't give you the C-47. If you didn't steal it, someone else did."

"I didn't steal it, you big ox-head. I found it and fixed it. But then I had to work for the U. S. so they wouldn't take it back from me."

"We'll figure it out." He pulled himself across the bed and leaned back on the headboard beside her.

They sat there, not speaking for several minutes. She tilted her head over onto his shoulder.

"How bad is it?"

"One prop flew off. It slid about 300 yards or so sideways. And it wasn't a soft landing."

"Maybe we can fix it." she looked across the room, thinking of her poor plane. Alone sitting in some dark field. Out of fuel and a broken prop.

Her head popped forward again. "Are those my guns?"

"Yes, the crate got broken open when we landed." He left out the part where Joey caved in the wooden case driving over it.

She let out a long sigh, "You guys really are going to get me killed." She went back to staring at the ceiling. "By the way, where are we?"

"I can only guess. Maybe fifty miles from Bacau, Romania."

"In which direction?" she started to calculate in her mind.

"South, mostly."

"You did good, Blejack." she smiled and slapped his arm several times before putting her hand back on her waist. "Only missed Bucharest by one fifty."

"If there is any credit, it is yours. I just kept it on your heading and hoped you had it where we needed it. You did good too." He rested his head on top of hers.

"What?"

"You didn't die on me."

"So, you were worried about me?"

"Of course I was worried." he grinned above her line of sight, "I didn't know how we were going to get home."

"Asshole!" She put her hand on the side of his face and shoved him away. "Go to the kitchen!"

He kept grinning, then grabbed her head with both hands and kissed her. "I worried about you every second."

Near Bacau, Romania.
February 8, 1945

MAEVE CHECKED THE MAP and compass and nodded to the others. They were on the right track. They had left the cabin at night, hoping to avoid any detection. Matty had fallen asleep, after she had given her some painkillers. Joey had volunteered to stay with her, and to guard the car. Paul had found a map in a secret compartment built into the kitchen cabinets. It showed the location of the Nazi base, and the surrounding area.

Jasper and Blejack had gathered some supplies and weapons and had briefed Erin and Paul on the plan. They had to reach the base and find a way to infiltrate it, and if possible, destroy it. They had to do it before the Nazis used their deadly weapons.

Jasper checked his watch and nodded to the others. It was time to go. They had spent three nights in the cabin, keeping Matty warm and comfortable. She insisted they go on. She would be fine, and this needed to be done as soon as possible. She had smiled and thanked Blejack, but she had also told him to go with the others and finish the mission. She knew how important it was.

Joey had protested, saying he wanted to help, but Jasper had convinced him that he was needed here. Blejack couldn't stay behind, he and Erin were their best hopes of relocating the hidden base. Someone had to stay with Matty and watch the car too.

The sun was rising, casting a pale light over the snow-covered forest. They followed a trail of footprints that they had spotted in the night, hoping it would lead them to the base. They moved quietly and cautiously, avoiding any open areas or signs of activity. The tracks disappeared at a small stream of cold clear water, so they continued forward through the trees toward where they thought the base would be.

They had been walking for about two hours, when they saw a sign. It was a wooden board, with skull and crossbones painted on it. It had a word written in German: Minen. Mines.

Maeve gasped and stopped. It was a minefield, probably planted by the Nazis to protect the base. They had to find a way to cross it, or they would never reach the base. She looked at her companions and signaled to them to be careful. She took out a knife and started to probe the ground in front of her. She hoped to find a safe path, or at least a gap in the mines. She moved slowly and cautiously and waited for the others to follow.

"Mom, just stop." Erin whispered.

Maeve froze in her tracks, worried that she had already put her foot onto one of the mines.

"Just back up, I have an idea that might go better."

Maeve let out a breath of relief. She stood up and looked behind her, carefully tracing her steps backward.

"Look, we lost those tracks at the stream, they went left or right, and I am going to guess left. That would lead them up into the hills further and not down toward the road. So, let's backtrack and go up the hill and around this. We are setting our own deadline right now. Let's not get in a hurry and make a mistake."

Everyone shook their heads in agreement. They backed away from the minefield and walked another 25 yards in the direction they had just come. Then they went to their right and up the hill, watching for the trail of footprints to reappear, crossing over in front of them.

About ten minutes later they were in luck. There was a well beaten path through the trees in front of them. They turned to the right again and followed the new trail.

They walked about a hundred yards when Erin held up her hand, stopping everyone. They all listened and could make out a low rumble, like an engine and faint voices.

She motioned with her hand for them to get down and pulled out a small pair of folding binoculars.

She could see a truck, painted in gray and black, with a swastika on the side. It had tracks on the rear instead of tires and it was parked on a narrow timber road that ran through the trees. There were two SS soldiers wearing winter uniforms and carrying rifles, leaning against the grill and talking.

She held up two fingers, informing the rest and waved them back to hide behind the trees.

Paul waved at Blejack, then pointed a finger at him and himself. Blejack nodded. They both dropped the packs they were carrying and opened their coats. Having clear access to their belts, they set off up the hill and moved toward the patrol.

The soldiers were both facing down the hill away from the truck, so Blejack and Paul worked their way behind it. They split up and waited at the corner. Paul shrugged, having nothing to go by, and pointed his thumb over his shoulder.

They both bent over and moved like big cats along the side of the truck.

At the rear of the cab, they could just barely see each other. Paul held up a long knife. Blejack showed him his own and nodded.

Each of them took a deep breath and moved silently forward.

Paul peeked over the hood and back down again. He looked on the ground for something, but there was only snow.

He dug through his pocket and found a large piece of hard candy. "I really wanted this for later," he thought. Then he threw it down the road hitting a tree trunk.

It made a small 'thunk' sound and got the soldiers' attention.

They stepped a few steps away from the truck, looking to see where the noise came from.

Paul and Blejack hustled the last few feet, each grabbing a man around his mouth and sliding their blades through their ribs.

Blejack gave the man's face a twist as he threw him to his left. The sound of his neck cracking only differed slightly from the sound of Paul's candy against the bark.

Paul whispered, "Knife wasn't good enough for you?"

"Double tap, manual style." He brushed away his partner's criticism.

"Not a terrible idea." Paul took his victim and used both hands, giving him a quick twist on the neck.

The two examined their work for a few seconds. There was some red snow, but not bad. Nothing that they couldn't scoop up.

"We had better put them in back of the truck." Paul suggested.

"Yeah, I guess." Blejack leaned over and pulled the man by his armpits. "Kind of makes me miss the Salamander."

"I was just going to say the same thing."

They teamed up on the limp bodies at the rear of the truck, then scooped up the blood stains and threw the tinted snow into the bed with the SS corpses.

Erin, Maeve, and Jasper came out of the trees at the half track as they closed up the tailgate.

They gathered around Maeve, who was holding up the map.

"Here, this is the timber road. But back around here, there is a mark. That isn't the base. What do you guys think it is?"

They looked at the page and then at the landscape, and it indicated a place behind the mountain that stood beyond the truck. The missile base was on the front side.

Erin took the map and looked closer.

"The people who made this map, they were doing recon. There is a reason they marked it there. I think we should check it out."

"Do you feel safe taking a look while Blejack and I get a look in front?" Jasper asked her.

"Don't leave me out. If you are going down the dragon's throat, I am going with you." Paul injected.

"I don't like the idea of leaving Erin and Maeve on their own." Jasper shook his head.

"Are you kidding?" Erin was almost shocked at her dad's statement. "You three 'man-children' go have your look and try to stay out of trouble. We don't need a man around to feel safe."

"That's not why I said that, Erin. You are my daughter. That is all I meant."

"Yeah, sure. Well, your family inherited everything you have, and then some. Just don't get yourselves captured and make me come bail you out."

Jasper sighed and nodded. He knew Erin was right. She was more than capable of taking care of herself and Maeve. She had proven that many times before. He also knew she was stubborn and independent, just like him. He couldn't stop her from doing what she wanted, even if he wanted to. He loved her and trusted her, but he also worried about her. He hoped she would be careful and cautious, and not take any unnecessary risks.

He checked out her radio and handed it back to her and said, "Here, keep this on. Keep in touch and let us know what you find. If you run into any trouble, call us and we'll come to help you. And if we run into any trouble, we'll do the same. Deal?"

Erin smiled and took the radio. She hugged her dad and said, "Deal. Don't worry, Dad. We'll be fine. You just focus on your mission and don't do anything stupid. And don't forget to have some fun. Who knows, you might get to blow some things up. You know how much you love that."

Jasper chuckled and said, "Yeah, I do. But not as much as you do. You're a chip off the old block, Erin. I'm proud of you."

He kissed her on the forehead and said, "Be safe, sweetheart. I love you."

"I love you too, Dad." Erin said.

She turned to Maeve and said, "Come on, Mom. Let's go see what's behind that mountain."

Maeve nodded and said, "Okay, honey. Let's go."

She hugged Jasper and said, "I love you, Jasper. Be careful."

"I love you too, Maeve. Anything looks like it is going to go sideways, you two get out of there, okay?" Jasper said.

He watched them walk away and couldn't help but be worried. Erin had been thrust into this new life and a world he had tried to shield her from since she was a baby. And Maeve, as strong as she was, was not the warrior breed. Now he had to let them go on their own into something none of them had any idea about.

He turned to Blejack and Paul and said, "All right, boys. Let's go see what's in front of that mountain."

Blejack grinned and said, "Let's go kick some Nazi ass.

Paul nodded and said, "Let's go make some history."

Jasper closed his eyes and shook his head. “Corny bastards.” He chuckled, “Just like old times.”

They moved through the trees, pausing behind a trunk or a rise in the ground, always checking their surroundings. When they reached the clearing that was nested up against the base of the mountain, they could see the complexity that was hidden there.

It was a multi-level concrete structure with a Panzer sitting on the top. Each level was stacked like a south American pyramid. There were nets strewn over the walls, helping to camouflage it from the air. There were several staff cars and other Nazi vehicles parked under hides between the trees and some upon the stepped roof of the bunker.

There were several gun emplacements on the upper levels. And an area like a garage where they could see some bundles and boxes inside.

At the base of the structure, there was a steel girder tower standing over a large hatch in the ground.

Jasper whispered, “They aren’t going to make it easy, are they?”

“Not this time.” Blejack answered him.

Jasper pointed toward the antenna tower, “You think you can take out their communications? That might even be part of their guidance system. We had better get rid of that first.”

“I was just about to suggest that myself,” Blejack smiled. “I will see you two shortly.”

He slid back away from the short bank and disappeared into the trees.

Jasper and Paul eased down and rolled onto their backs.

"It's all over but the doing, isn't it Paul?"

"Seems like it."

"What do you think?" Jasper could see this was no simple war.

"I see two guards up there. One on the top and one below. I could take them both with this rifle before they had time to scratch their ass."

"Yeah, I know you could. But that is going to alert everyone inside and we would never get in. We are going to have to go in quiet, somehow."

They rolled back on their stomachs and peeked over the edge, taking in the polished black boots standing right in front of their noses.

The German soldiers pointed their rifles at Jasper and Paul and shouted: "Legt eure Waffen nieder! Sofort!" (Drop your weapons! Now!)

Jasper and Paul looked at each other and realized they were had. They had no choice but to comply. They slowly dropped their guns and raised their hands.

Jasper felt his small radio in his pocket, and he tapped on the speaker, sending the signal to Erin. But would the signal reach them? That was a coin toss. These were designed for short range and not going through mountains of rock.

The German soldiers approached them and kicked their weapons away. They searched them and took their radios and their knives. They said: "Wer seid ihr? Was macht ihr hier?" (Who are you? What are you doing here?)

Jasper and Paul didn't answer. They knew they were in trouble. They hoped that Blejack was still alive and that he could warn Erin and Maeve.

The German soldiers grabbed them by their arms and dragged them towards the bunker. They continued in German "You're coming with us. The commander will deal with you."

The German soldiers dragged Jasper and Paul into the bunker. They walked through the dark and narrow corridors, passing by several doors and rooms. They saw wires and pipes running along the walls and ceiling. They heard the hum of machines and the buzz of radios. The place smelled of metal and oil and sweat.

They reached a large metal door with a sign that read, "Kommandozentrale" (Command Center). The soldiers knocked on the door and said, "Herr Kommandant, we have two prisoners. They tried to attack the base."

The door opened and a man in a black uniform and a peaked cap came out. He had a stern face and a thin mustache. He wore a pair of binoculars around his neck and a pistol on his belt. He was the commanding officer of the missile base. He looked at Jasper and his friend and said, "What were they doing? Where did you find them?"

The soldiers saluted and said, "We don't know, sir. They have no papers or dog tags. They only have these weapons and these small radios."

The commanding officer took the radios and examined them. He had never seen such small radios. He said, "They are spies. They are here for sabotage or to reveal our location to the allies."

He turned to Jasper and Paul and said, "Sprechen sie Deutsch? Englisch? Französisch?" (Do you speak German? English? French?)

Jasper and Paul didn't answer. They knew saying anything would only speed up their end. They hoped that Erin and Maeve had heard their message and that they were safe.

The commanding officer frowned and said, "You don't want to talk? Good. Then I will make you talk. Bring them."

He led them into a room that only had a few chairs and the guards shoved them inside and slammed the door behind them locking it.

They had no idea how long they had waited there. Jasper had just lost his faithful watch to that SS dirt-bag. And he had every intention of getting it back. Somehow.

MEANWHILE, ERIN AND Maeve followed the map and the trail, heading towards the rear of the mountain. They moved stealthily and quietly, staying to the trees. They knew they were close to the enemy territory, and they didn't want to alert them to their presence.

They reached a small clearing, where they saw a large archway carved into the rock. It was partially covered by brush and snow and ice, but they could see that it was a tunnel leading into the mountain. Hanging from the wall was a sign that read, "Achtung! Sperrgebiet! Zutritt verboten!" which meant, "Attention! Restricted area! No entry!"

Erin looked at Maeve and said, "Well, this must be it. This is what they marked on the map. A back door to the base."

Maeve looked at the sign and said, "Or a trap. Maybe they knew someone would find this and try to get in. Maybe they have guards or mines or booby traps waiting for us."

Erin shrugged and said, "Maybe. But there's only one way to find out. And we're not going to let a little sign stop us, are we?"

Erin looked around the edges of the big steel door, trying to find the locking mechanism. Maeve kept her eyes out behind and around them. Then the small radio made its chattering noise indicating they were receiving a message.

She tapped the speaker and heard voices speaking in German.

“Didn’t I tell them not to get captured, mom? If I told them a hundred times, I told them once.”

“You did, and that is not really how that expression goes.”

“Well, we are out of time to mess with this door. I am going in my way. Move back.”

Her eyes lit up and the blue current began to wash over her arms and hands. She let it build for a few seconds then placed both hands on the door.

There was a loud squealing sound and the door exploded sending shrapnel down through the dark tunnel. The mountain shook and dust rolled out the doorway.

Erin walked through the opening, shining the way before her. Maeve followed, bringing some light of her own. She had extended a shield around the pair of them

Erin’s hands were held out to her sides, electricity flowing against both walls as she walked.

The tunnel went in about a hundred yards then split off, going into a circle around the center of the bunker. There were doors just around the corner in each direction that led to the middle.

“The doors look like a shorter walk.” Erin said.

"No use in dawdling. After you."

The light made a high pitched sound as Erin swept her hands from the walls to the door, blasting it off its hinges and into the opening.

She walked through into a large conference room with a low ceiling. The few soldiers that were there began to step up like they planned to put up a fight, then they saw the reality of their situation and ran out the door on the other end.

Erin and Maeve calmly walked through the room. An occasional head popped out of a doorway on one side or the other, then slipped right back out of the room.

They went through the doorway at the opposite end to find another large room. It looked like a cafeteria. The sound of sliding chairs was immediate and the men who sat in them had no illusions. They got up and ran out whichever door was closest to them.

They passed through this room like the other, with no resistance. The door at the end of this room passed through a small kitchen and storage area. Then out into the other end of the circling tunnels.

Stepping out into the narrow passage, Erin saw another door. If she calculated right, it should lead beneath the launch tower she and Blejack had seen in front of the bunker.

"Mom, I hope dad can hold out. We need to go down and disable those missiles."

"I am sure he can string them along. If we don't stop these now, we might not get another chance."

Erin used her master key and opened the doorway. They ran down a flight of stairs that turned at the bottom and went back the other way. When they reached the bottom there was a long steel catwalk. They both landed their feet on it and turned back toward the front of the bunker.

Now they could see it. Far below the catwalk there was a big circular concrete pad with huge vent tubes around it. On top of it was a missile with lines attached to it in several places.

The room was massive. The floor below was easily 70 feet from them. The catwalk extended all the way around, with several stairwells and steel ladders extending down.

Between the standing missile and themselves was a large steel barrier that separated the one on the pad from a row of replacements.

There was a large rail system and hydraulic machines that they used to move these monsters. Little men below in white coats went on with their work, not yet noticing them.

"Well, It is a long walk down there, mom."

Maeve tipped her head over the rail, giving it all a second look.

"Yes, it is that."

"I don't feel like walking. I think I will just fix it up from here."

"If I can help, just tell me." Maeve wasn't that fond of heights. She had eased herself back away from the outer edge of the catwalk.

"Not sure if we need it or if it would help, but go ahead and put that ball of light around us. I am going to lay their missile down right in their road. Then I am going to break the bottom off so they can't ever stand it up again."

Maeve put out her sphere of light around them both and Erin went to work.

She sent her fiery tentacles out and around the top of the missile and brought it down on top of several of the men below. Others had finally noticed her now, and were running to avoid being crushed.

Then she cut the bottom of the missile open, spilling it's fuel and guts into the dark floor. Alarms began to go off, wailing repetitively throughout the bunker. Flashing lights above and below them.

"That should keep them. Let's go get dad and Paul and Blejack."

They both turned and ran back up the stairwell.

TWO SS SOLDIERS OPENED their cell and led them back to the command center.

There were metal cabinets around the walls, covered with dials, switches, knobs and what must have been counters. They had rows of black numbers on a white background covered with clear glass lenses. It was easy to see these would be the controls for the missiles.

The commander was sitting at a large table where they saw a map. On the map, there were big red circles around Moscow, London and Washington DC. It was also obvious these cities were their targets.

He looked around and saw several other officers and technicians working in the room. They looked at Jasper and his friends with curiosity and hostility. They whispered among themselves and said things like, "Who are these guys? What are they up to? How did they manage to get here?"

The commanding officer brought Jasper and his friends to the table and said, "See this map? See these targets? These are the cities that we will destroy. We have the most powerful weapons in the world. We have the V2 missiles. They are fast, accurate and deadly. They can reach any city in Europe or America. They can win the war for Germany. They can conquer the world for Hitler."

Another man stood next to the commander. This one was in all black. Gestapo.

"I know you two speak English. We don't have time for games." He pointed to the table where the tiny radios and Paul's revolver were lying. He picked up the gun and opened it, removing all but one bullet.

"So, which one of you is going to talk to me?"

He spun the cylinder, held it up and fired it at Jasper's forehead.

Jasper blinked his eyes and held his ground.

"Maybe it will be you? You are familiar with this game?"

He gave the gun another spin and raised it to Paul's head and the gun gave another resounding click.

Jasper would take his own chances, but he wouldn't take them with Paul. "What is it you think we can tell you?"

The Gestapo officer smiled and said, "You can tell me a lot of things. You can tell me who you are, where you come from, what you want, who sent you, who else knows about this base, and how you found out about it. You can tell me everything I need to know, or you can die. The choice is yours."

He spun the cylinder again and pointed the gun at Jasper's chest. He said, "Let's start with the basics. Who are you?"

Jasper looked at him and said, "I'm nobody. Just a traveler. I'm here to see the sights, to enjoy the scenery, and to admire the culture."

The Gestapo officer laughed and said, "Don't lie to me. I thought we were past the games. You're a spy. You're a saboteur. You're here to destroy our base, to stop our missiles, to ruin our plans. You're here to make me trouble."

He pointed the gun at Jasper's leg this time. He pulled the trigger and the gun clicked again.

"You're lucky. But your luck won't last. Let's get to the meat of it, shall we? Who else knows we are here and who sent you?"

He put a finger on the gun's cylinder and gave it one click, then held it pointed at Paul's head.

"First, I don't think you are playing this game right. And second, I don't think you plan on letting us live much longer than the moment we step out of this room. But to answer your question, we just found you here. No one sent us. We were doing something else, and it all went sideways. You were just a lucky accident."

"There, now we are getting someplace. What is your name?" He put his left arm behind his back, pacing proudly behind the table.

"Jasper Carrigan."

The look of recognition came onto the officer's face like a light bulb had been turned on in his brain.

"Tie their hands." he yelled to the guards.

"And this one, he must be the one they call Paul Bunyan?"

Paul's brow curled, "No one calls me that."

The guards tied both their hands and shoved them down into a pair of chairs.

"That brings me another question to mind," the little Hitler pawn went on. "Where are your friends? Where is Blee jack?"

A low rumbling sound began to resonate through the walls and floor of the room. Red lights flashed on the panels around them. The sound of an explosion roared into their ears and concrete and rock dust clogged their throats.

"Looks like they came with us."

Men started shouting behind the Gestapo officer in German. They pulled on switches and turned dials and pointed at the timers.

The missile was set to launch in five minutes and the doors wouldn't open.

A phone rang on the commander's desk. Someone on the other end warned him that the missile had fallen over on the launch pad.

The Gestapo officer flared at them. "I want to shoot both of you so badly right now. But I think I will give you something better. I will lock you in with the bombs. You will like them. They are atomic bombs."

Jasper shrugged. "We figured on going today one way or another."

The commander and the gestapo agent both took turns yelling and men were running through the tunnels and out the doors.

"Get them out of my sight! Put them back in the cell! And keep them there!"

Jasper reached forward and snatched his watch off the table as the two guards jostled them out of the chairs and back into the hallway.

The men in the command center tried desperately to shut down the launch sequence. But nothing was responding. First one, then several ran for the door and out of the tunnel.

Outside cars were being started and men running to them as they pulled away. The tunnel filled with voices of soldiers and scientists trying to escape the coming blast. Several rushed past them as Jasper and Paul were led back to the concrete room. Their faces were covered in terror.

"Paul, looks like we might be out of luck this time."

"It isn't over until it's over, Jasper."

The guards opened the door and gave them a push inside.

"Assholes." Jasper got off as they shut the door.

Then they heard the sound of gunfire in the hall. A couple of shots, then more. Then the sound of hinges squeaking and Blejack's face poking through the opening.

"You two rested up yet? Or do you need a few minutes?"

"You are right on time. We need to get Maeve and Erin and get the hell out of here. We are all about to be cooked in an explosion like nothing this earth has seen before." Jasper held out his hands for Blejack to cut him loose.

He made fast work of the binding, "Go, go get the girls. We will meet you out front."

Jasper stepped through the door, reached down and took a sub-machine gun from one of the Nazi bodies and broke down the long tunnel looking for his wife and daughter.

A FEW SECONDS LATER Erin and Maeve came running toward him in the dim light.

"Come on, we have to go now. The place is going to blow," he yelled at them.

Jasper turned and ran with them for the exit.

When they got out the main door they kept running, he tried to talk and run, but he gave up.

"Stop a second. We aren't going to get far enough away. I have seen this kind of explosion before."

The three of them stopped.

"Come here, let me just hold you two for a minute. We only have a few left before this goes off. The problem with nuclear weapons is that when you destroy them, you are likely to destroy a good part of the earth with them."

"Well, we aren't going to just stand here and wait for it." Maeve kisses Jasper and Erin. "Run. Get as far as you can. I am going to control this."

"No, Maeve, you don't know how powerful this is. It will be like a million of those V2 bombs."

"Erin, take him. Make him go with you. This is my time to do. Jasper, we do what we can when we can. We have lived by that code. You take our baby out of here now."

She turned and walked away from them, back to the bunker.

She began to glow white. A large orb began to grow out in front of her.

Erin pulled on Jasper. "Let's go. She is the only one that can do this."

Jasper couldn't bring himself to walk away from his wife.

"Blejack! Paul! Help me here!" Erin yelled.

Jasper's old friends stopped and turned back, running to help Erin force Jasper away from the coming blast.

"I can't leave her alone!" Jasper barked.

"You do as she asked!" Erin snapped back. "Grab his damn arms and make him move, will you?"

Blejack looked at Jasper, "Come on, Cappy. It's time to go. Don't make us grab you."

He looked back at Blejack and Erin and Paul, then submitted to their demands.

"Run!" Erin shouted, "Run as fast as you can!"

She slapped her dad on the back, "You too. Now!"

They ran. And as fast as they could. But they didn't even make the tree line.

The ground shook so hard that they all fell from their feet and slid down the slope toward the forest.

Maeve held her arms out, holding the huge sphere of white light around the explosions. The Earth continued to shake beneath them all, and there was a loud moaning sound, like a strong wind blowing across the end of a long tunnel.

She fell to her knees, struggling against the flames that filled the globe. Her eyes closed and she concentrated everything she had inside of her holding back the starburst torrents that raged against her.

Her body was glowing white through her clothes and the red stripped away from her hair leaving it white as the snow below her.

With a loud and sudden vacuum sound, she fell to the earth completely and the shield vanished.

Everything inside the huge ring was gone. Only black soil and burned concrete remained of the missile base. Sandstone rocks melted into chaotic globs of glass. Clouds of ash drifted into the wind.

Erin ran to her mother, pulling her from the ground. There was no breath. No heartbeat. No light in her eyes.

She pulled her limp body to her chest, crying, "No! No! Mama, you don't get to go! You don't get to leave me!"

Tears rolled down her face and she held her mother up from below her arm, pressing her mom's chest to her own. Her other hand holding her head to her shoulder, she tilted her head forward kissing her forehead, begging her to come back.

Jasper picked himself up and, his own eyes now wet with pain, walked to his daughter and his lost love. How could he live without her? How could he wake up in an empty world?

Blejack and Paul began to stand up, everyone had been knocked down by the blast. They followed Jasper. They all tried to choke back the tears.

"Erin, honey, let me have her?" Jasper asked.

Erin shook her head and pulled her closer.

"Erin, please? Let me hold her."

She looked up with her bloodshot eyes and saw the tears running down his face.

She shook her head, "Okay." she stuttered and sniffed.

Jasper put his arms around Maeve and Erin released her.

He sat down, holding her head in his lap, his tears raining down on her cheeks. He thought about the lagoon. "We could stay." she had said.

His voice made a choking sound as he tried to hold back his pain.

Erin stepped backwards, stumbling as she went, blinded by her tears.

She couldn't believe this. She wouldn't. She wouldn't accept this. Her whole life, her mother had only saved people. She stitched them and comforted them and fed them. Whatever powers the gods had given her, she only used to save other people.

Her mind raced from one thought to the next, like jumping across rocks in a shallow stream.

She watched her dad's heart breaking, and the men she knew all her life crying openly for the first time. And her mom, laying there dead.

"No! No!" She repeated, getting louder. "No!"

She turned back to the demolished base and saw red taillights racing away in the dark.

All at once, she turned into a bright blue fire. Not just her hands or arms or eyes. Her whole body.

Her broad wings burst from her back in a flash of light. A gold crown wrapped itself around her head with small wings above her ears. Her ankles and wrists were wrapped in gold bands. Her chest was covered in gold and silver armor. Around her waist was a broad leather belt with long plates of gold embossed leather hanging over ribbons of silk cloth, blowing in the wind below.

She took a step and threw her arms up, soaring into the wind a hundred feet above them.

She watched the Nazis trying to run away. Thought about what she had been told. "No one could know. There are repercussions."

But she didn't care. No one would know. No one was going to walk away tonight. She was the repercussion. She would be judgment.

She leaned back and let out a cry that became a scream. The sky covered itself with clouds and thunder.

The fiery blue that ran up and down Erin's body began to expand in front of her. She rolled back, looking like a fallen angel from some classic painting.

Her voice filled the air with her pain and anger, and the flame soared across the terrain in front of her. It raced up into the stratosphere and across the land, tearing down anything in its path.

Trees blew out of the landscape and laid down like a volcanic wind had thrown them there, with their torn and broken roots exposed. Cars and trucks burst into flames. They went from speeding down the road to a rolling stop, as the rubber tires turned to smoke. Then the metal itself turned to ash.

The men in their black uniforms ran through the dark, screaming as they too felt her touch. They were blown to the ground, then crushed by the wave and lit like torches, turning to dust.

The sky went neon blue for miles in front of her. Lightning tore through the clouds, reinforcing her decision. She thought to herself, "Zeus himself will know fear tonight."

She unleashed a hurricane of fire and death before her. "There will be repercussions." Trees turned to long lines of ash. Nothing before her would survive her loss.

And a single strand of light, like a wire that had been bent and unrolled and bent again before it was stretched back out, ran from her feet to the ground.

It moved at a crawl until it found Maeve's body. When it reached the center of her chest, it stopped there.

Both Blejack and Jasper were still holding her and were both frozen in place, paralyzed.

There was a loud whooshing sound, a humming noise, and then a loud cracking. And Erin fell, turning in the air until she dropped onto the ground.

Paul was still stunned. He took a step away from Maeve and ran toward Erin to see if she was okay.

Then behind him, someone began coughing. He looked back to see Maeve open her eyes.

She had a stunned look on her face, as she tried to get her bearings and catch her breath.

Paul turned back to Erin. She tried to lift herself onto her elbows, then folded her arms and dropped her head back down.

She lay there on her side, her wings still spread out behind her, looking literally like a fallen angel.

Erin grabbed her head and squinted her eyes, now blackened around the edges. Long trails of soot marked the path of her tears.

Maeve began to sit up, and Jasper helped lift her to her feet.

"Erin, are you okay?" She asked, seeing her daughter still on the ground.

Erin just lay there. "Mom, I think I'm hurt."

Maeve walked quickly over to her baby girl, her feet crunching in the snow. She sat down next to her and pulled her gently onto her lap. She put her arms around her and began petting her hair like a small kitten.

"I can't get up." Erin almost whispered.

Maeve held her daughter's head to her chest, "It's okay, baby. We will take care of you."

"I love you, mom." she said, muffled against Maeve's breast.

"I know you do, hon. I love you too. Just relax. We will get you home, won't we, Jasper?"

Jasper sat down next to Maeve, and the others gathered around her in a small circle.

"Of course we will. We just need to get you out of the cold, and then we will start making our way back home."

Behind them all, small clouds of mist began to appear: Aphrodite, Athena, Eris, and a new face, Paean, the doctor of the gods.

Erin's eyes felt on fire and her vision was blurred, but she could make the man out. He had wings like hers. He was physically strong and had short black hair. His chest was covered in armor and his arms and legs wore matching bracers and anklets.

They all walked up, with serious looks on their faces.

Paean leaned down and examined her, then they crowded in, pushing back the crew as he lifted Erin off the ground.

"Erin, this can never happen. Control. That was the first thing I told you. You can't ever let go of it." Aphrodite chastised her young granddaughter.

They could all hear the anger, frustration and fear in her voice.

Eris glanced at Maeve, "We have to take her with us."

"No! You can't take her from us!" Maeve exclaimed, horrified by what she was hearing.

"We must take her now. There is no time. What she did just now. That was too much." Eris snapped.

"What did she do?" Maeve asked, confused. She had no idea what had happened. She had no idea that moments ago she was lying dead in Jasper's arms.

"She gave her life to you." Eris said, softly.

Maeve tried to spark up her shield and stop them from taking Erin away.

"It's over, Maeve," Eris said to her, "It's all gone."

Maeve teared up and looked at Jasper, pleading with her eyes for him to do something, say something.

Jasper was lost inside. He had trusted Aphrodite for a long time now. She wouldn't let them down, would she?

"Are you going to help her?" Blejack asked Eris firmly.

"We are going to try." Eris looked straight into his eyes. "She crossed a lot of lines. She has balls, that's for sure. It is going to take all of us to keep her out of trouble upstairs."

Finally, Jasper got his voice, "What lines? Her mom died trying to save half the planet, and she killed a bunch of Nazi SS scumbags. I see no lines crossed there."

Eris leaned in and pulled him close to her and whispered, "She threatened Zeus while she was doing it. Not even Poseidon would dare to do that."

"Well, she is only human. We have a tendency to say things out of anger and pain that we wouldn't say under normal circumstances." Jasper appealed to Eris for his girl.

"I know that. That is why we are going to take her. You have to let us work this one out." Eris gave him a wink and whispered again, "Athena will wear him down."

"I heard that, but she is right." Athena called to them from beside the doctor, not lifting her gaze from Erin.

Maeve reached out and took Eris's arm to get her attention, "So, we are normal now?"

Eris shook her head yes. "Sis, you cheated Hades. You are lucky to be standing here right now. He is probably throwing a god sized tantrum down there."

The doctor cut himself into the conversation, "We are running out of time, ladies. We need to get her back to my place."

Aphrodite stepped over and held Maeve, "I'm sorry. They need to tell you the rest. We do have to go now." She kissed Maeve on her forehead d, "I do love you."

Aphrodite circled her arm into the air, and they were all gone in a fog.

"Jasper," Blejack got his cousin's attention, and held his hand out in front of his stomach, rolling his thumb across his fingertips. Little blue sparks jumped across them. "I don't think we are all normal."

Jasper looked down at his own hand and copied Blejack's movements. Little blue sparks.

"Well, that is something, isn't it." He said, surprised.

Blejack winked at him and smiled.

"Maeve, let's go home." He put his arm around her shoulder.

"I can't wait to leave this god forsaken place, Jasper." She said, relieved.

Epilogue

Limburg, Germany.
March 27, 1945

Erin put it all out of her mind. The world had changed, and she had changed since that day.

She crouched behind a pile of rubble, watching the German tanks and soldiers firing at the American positions. She could hear the screams and explosions, and anger and revulsion coursed through her. She had been on the sidelines of this war for too long, and she had seen too much death and suffering. Now she could help, she could end this.

She looked around, making sure no one was watching her. She waited for the right moment, when the German fire was most intense, and the American troops were most vulnerable. She saw a gap in the enemy lines, and she ran for it. She moved fast, dodging the bullets and shells, and reached the other side. She found a spot behind a burned-out car, and she prepared to unleash her power. She sat down and leaned back as blue electric flames began to pour through the tiny pores in her skin. Wrapping up her forearms.

She raised her hand and felt the electricity coursing through her veins. She aimed at the nearest German tank and released a bolt of blue fire. The tank exploded, sending shrapnel and flames in all directions. She smiled and moved on to the next target. She repeated the process, destroying one tank after another, creating a path of destruction and chaos.

She didn't stop there. She saw a group of German soldiers hiding behind a wall, and she threw another bolt of fire at them. The wall collapsed, crushing and burning the soldiers. She saw a German officer on a balcony, shouting orders and pointing a pistol. She threw another bolt of fire at him, hitting him in the chest. He fell, his body smoking and charred.

She felt a rush of adrenaline and satisfaction, and she could hear the American troops far behind her. They were advancing, taking advantage of the confusion and panic she had caused. The sudden break in artillery fire on their positions and explosions outside of their view must have put questions in their mind, but they weren't waiting for the answers.

She didn't stay to watch, though. She knew she had to leave, before anyone noticed her. She ran back to the other side, avoiding the enemy fire and the friendly fire alike. She reached her hiding spot, and she breathed a sigh of relief. She had done it. They would be able to move in and take this city now.

She shook her head and wiped the sweat and dirt from her face. She didn't have time to wonder. She had to keep moving and keep fighting.

She was in Berlin, the capital of Nazi Germany, and the final battleground of World War 2. It was April 1945, and the Allies were closing in on the city from all sides. The Soviet Red Army was advancing from the east, and the British and American forces were advancing from the west. The German resistance was fierce, but futile. The city was doomed, and so was the Nazi regime.

Just a few months ago, she was a simple aid inside the British SIS. She wasn't an agent. But she had played the part. That is how she got here now. And it was time to go. Time to get out of this city and meet up with Joey and Eris.

She approached the open door, hanging from its lower hinge. There was broken glass and debris scattered on the floor and large sections of wall were missing and distributed among the burned and broken furnishings in the room.

She could hear the tanks chattering and rumbling down the street and peeked past the edge of the broken wall to see.

Three Panzer tanks, pointing their guns toward each side and forward.

She stepped back and the blue flames in her hands began to grow. Moving up her arms. Her eyes started to blaze and blue threads of electricity formed almost a bird's shape on her upper chest. Trails of the bright light began to trace itself down her cheekbones from the corners of her eyes.

She stepped out the door, noises crackling from her body as she released a stream of fire. There was a loud hum as the bolt surged down the street. The smell of burning elements.

The first tank took the hit on its nose, then the current jumped into the second and third all in the same instant.

The three tanks exploded sending shards of torn and melted steel through the air, mixed with tiny pieces of the men who had been inside them.

She looked around and dashed across the street into another building and continued through, using her power to open a hole in the wall at the rear.

She emerged from the building and ran towards the outskirts of the city, where she hoped to find a vantage point to see the camp. She knew it was close, but she didn't know exactly where. She had been searching for weeks, following the clues and the rumors, hoping to find her family alive. She had left Paean's mountain hideaway after the bunker incident, knowing that she had to get away from the goddesses who were now hunting her. She had also left behind a part of herself, a part that she didn't want to face yet.

She had traveled across Germany, hiding her identity and her powers, blending in with the refugees and the resistance. She had seen the horrors of the war, the death and the destruction, the cruelty and the despair. She had also seen hope and courage, kindness and sacrifice, love and loyalty. She had met many people along the way, some who helped her, some who hindered her, some who became her friends, some who became her enemies. She had learned a lot about herself and the world, but she had also lost a lot along the way.

She had one goal in mind: to find her family and reunite with them. She had heard that they had been captured by the Nazis and taken to a POW camp somewhere in Germany.

She had tried to locate them for weeks, but she had to be careful not to draw too much attention to herself.

She had to avoid the goddesses, who could sense her presence and her power.

She had to avoid the Nazis, who could recognize her face and her name because of the moles at the SIS.

She had to avoid the Allies, who had mistaken her for an enemy and would shoot her on sight.

She had to avoid everyone, except her parents and her friends.

Erin reached the edge of the city and climbed a hill, where she could see a large fence with barbed wire and guard towers.

There were rows of wooden barracks and tents, where hundreds of men in ragged uniforms were crowded together.

Drifting in the breeze above was a flag with a red cross, indicating that this was a POW camp.

Her heart pulsed with emotion, a mix of relief and fear, of joy and sorrow, of hope and dread.

Were Jasper and Maeve still there?

Were they still alive?.

Also by J. J. Caler

Jasper And The Salamander[1]
Erin Rise[2]
Bring it Back (Coming Soon)

1. https://www.draft2digital.com/catalog/1268833
2. https://www.draft2digital.com/catalog/1271884

Don't miss out!

Visit the website below and you can sign up to receive emails whenever J. J. Caler publishes a new book. There's no charge and no obligation.

https://books2read.com/r/B-A-VEADB-QMJUC

BOOKS 2 READ

Connecting independent readers to independent writers.

Also by J. J. Caler

Jasper And The Salamander
Erin Rise

Milton Keynes UK
Ingram Content Group UK Ltd.
UKHW020657260224
438492UK00017B/859